THE
Dowager's Daughter

MONA PREVEL

DIVERSIONBOOKS

Also by Mona Prevel

A Kiss for Lucy
Educating Emily
The Love-Shy Lord

Diversion Books
A Division of Diversion Publishing Corp.
443 Park Avenue South, Suite 1008
New York, New York 10016
www.DiversionBooks.com

For more information, email info@diversionbooks.com

First Diversion Books edition April 2014.
Print ISBN: 978-1-62681-680-0
eBook ISBN: 978-1-62681-272-7

Dedicated to those three handsome devils:
My sons, Stephen, Charles, and Richard.

Chapter 1

Unaware that she was doing so, Althea Markham tapped her foot to the strains of a lilting tune emanating from the musicians' gallery. She watched the elegantly attired couples dance by her chair, the gauzy dresses of the ladies reminding her of butterflies in flight.

Even when asked to dance, Althea did not feel that she belonged with such a glittering throng, but rather, was an outsider who had wandered by chance into their midst. It was as if there were a secret password that allowed one into their inner circle—and she did not know it.

She frowned slightly when a woman with flame-colored hair came into view, her slender form held firmly by the white-gloved hand of Marcus Ridley. He was considered one of the most handsome men in England, and where the fairer sex was concerned, definitely the most dangerous. Females, it was rumored, surrendered their virtue to him with the reckless abandon of lemmings hurling themselves to their doom—without even the slightest suggestion on his part that marriage might be included in the arrangement.

Althea's gaze shifted back and forth between the pair. The woman was one of those fortunate redheads in possession of exquisite features and a rose petal complexion. She was a fitting consort for the dark-haired, blue-eyed Viscount Ridley, son and heir of the Earl of Fairfax, and evidently knew it, for she appeared to have the upper hand in the exchange of flirtatious glances passing between them.

Even so, Althea thought, *have a care, darling; duels of the heart can be every bit as lethal as those on the grass at dawn.*

She drew in her breath as the viscount whispered in his

partner's ear. Seemingly without giving his words a moment's consideration, the feckless creature nodded and they disappeared through the French doors leading to the terrace.

Althea's foot ceased its tapping and her forehead furrowed in dismay. "Oh, dear," she muttered under her breath. "Celeste Markham, I fear you have just torn what was left of your reputation to shreds. How too, too mortifying."

Althea rose from her chair, snapped closed the ivory handles to her silk fan with an angry flick of her wrist, and departed the elegant rose-and-gilt ballroom.

She was tempted to desert her guests and repair to her chambers, but good manners prevailed and she retired to the comfort of the library, telling herself that as soon as she had regained her composure, she would return to their midst.

There were no candles lit, but the room was afforded a dim light from the glow of a slowly dying fire, so she felt her way to a leather wingback chair, invitingly obscured by shadows.

Althea had calmed down almost to the point of dozing off, when the creak of the opening door brought her fully awake. She was about to make her presence known to the intruder when a masculine voice with the affected drawl of a Corinthian dandy caused her to wince.

"You owe me twenty gold ones, Lampton old chap. Did I not say that Ridley would inveigle Celeste Markham to toss her petticoats before the dance was over?"

The tall, too-slender silhouette of the speaker could only be that of George Delville—one whom, up to that moment, Althea had considered to be a friend. She clenched her fists until her fingernails dug into the palms of her hands. How dare he speak in such a fashion about a member of her family while partaking of her hospitality!

"I suppose I do." The one addressed as Lampton sighed. "Just a few words in her ear was all it took—and right in the middle of the dance, they both hared out to the garden like a pair of puppies in first heat. How does he do it, Delville? I mean to say—the lady is a diamond of the first water."

"I must concur. The lady in question is indeed one of

Society's loveliest flowers. Especially remarkable when one considers the fiery color of her hair. It has been my experience that women with ginger hair usually have ruddy complexions and faces like horses. Hortense Lavendar comes to mind."

Francis Lampton shuddered. "Pray do not remind me. My father did his damnedest to leg-shackle me to Miss Lavendar. Her sire offered considerable acreage abutting his estate and ours as an inducement. The rich mushroom was willing to pay dearly to make his daughter the next Baroness Lampton."

Delville accorded his friend a sympathetic cluck.

Lampton shuddered. "I break into a cold sweat every time I think of it." He peered around the room. "So where does the old uncle keep his cognac? I must say, it's as dark as a crypt in here."

"For pity's sake, that is easily rectified." Delville bustled past his friend and stoked the fire into a sputtering flame, then took a wooden spill from a receptacle on the hearth and thrust it into the fire.

"There!" He turned, his hand cupped around the spill to protect the wavering flicker of light, and gave an impatient click of his tongue. "Pray make yourself useful and hand me a candlestick. It is deucedly drafty in here."

Lampton peered around, removed a candelabrum boasting five sconces from a nearby desk, and thrust it toward Delville. "Here. There is no need to be so testy about it."

"Sorry about that. It was unintentional." Delville lit the candles and walked over to one of the booklined walls. "I say, such weighty tomes—and well-handled, by the looks of it. I am afraid that the present Countess of Camberly is too serious by half. Title notwithstanding, no wonder she is still unclaimed, and this being her fourth Season."

Lampton snickered. "No matter how great her beauty, the wanton ways of Celeste Markham would deter all but the most desperate of adventurers. Make a chap think twice before taking her to wife. I had intended to pay her court. Rather fancied the idea of having a son inherit an earldom—especially from such a beautiful mother. But as it is, my heir shall have to make do with a barony." He laughed. "With such a jade, one could not claim with any certainty to have sired *any* of her children."

The flames sputtered in the grate, revealing the ample form and ruddy complexion of Baron Lampson's heir.

Delville shook his head. "If you did not bury yourself in the country from one year to the next, you would not be laboring under such a misapprehension."

"What are you babbling about?"

"Celeste Markham's beauty belies her years, but even if it were still possible for her to breed—that, I cannot say—you still would not get an earl on her. She is the *dowager* of the family. Her daughter, Althea, is the present Countess of Camberly. Surely you were presented to her upon arriving this evening?"

"Can't say as I was. I put in a deucedly late appearance and she was not in evidence. Probably fussing over the refreshments or visiting the necessary, I should imagine."

"Quite so."

"Pray tell me the daughter does not demonstrate her mother's wanton ways."

"There is not a whisper of scandal attached to her name, but I doubt our Althea has been put to the test."

Delville's patronizing tone caused Althea to grit her teeth.

"Oh?" Disappointment weighed heavily on Lampton's voice. "The countess is an antidote? Favors her father, then? I have heard the late earl was a dry old bird, more given to poring over musty books than to gaming and chasing the ladies."

Althea's body tensed. She dreaded to hear Delville's assessment of what he no doubt considered to be her meager charms. It would have been far, far better had she done the proper thing and made her presence known to the interlopers before the situation had deteriorated into such a nightmare.

Delville stroked his chin. "Considering she is only twenty-one, she is somewhat lacking in style—wears her hair in a tight little bun, and dresses more like a dowdy governess than a titled lady of great fortune—but an antidote? I would not go so far as to call her such. Her features do not command attention one way or the other—except, perhaps, her eyes ..."

"Her eyes?" A glimmer of hope colored Lampson's tone.

"Yes. They are quite large, and an unusual shade of green. Rather like moonstones in a tide-pool."

"I say. That *is* a trifle fanciful. You would not be harboring a *tendre* for the lady yourself, by any chance?"

"Absolutely not. As far as I am concerned she is completely lacking in the feminine charm that I require in a wife."

"I will not let such a detail deter me from my intent. Soften her with wine, divest her of her nightshift and douse the lights, and I daresay I should find the marriage bed quite tolerable."

"What a noble chappie you are." Delville affected a dramatic sigh. "Willing to sacrifice yourself on the altar of matrimony to further the fortunes of a brat who is yet to be born. Ah! Here it is."

"Here's what?"

Delville held a decanter aloft. "The Marquis de Maligny's cognac. The wily old Frenchman had it tucked away in this cabinet." Delville placed the candelabrum on the cabinet and returned to the fireplace. "I believe you will find some glasses on that table beside you, old chap."

Lampton gave a dismissive wave. "Forget about the cognac. I would far rather return to the ballroom. I should like you to present me to our hostess, and if I find her looks in the least tolerable, I shall make a point of attending her next 'at home.'"

"That would be Wednesday. But a word to the wise, old chap."

"Hmmm?"

"Prepare yourself for a tedious and arduous courtship."

"How so?"

"I rather suspect the lady is looking for true love and is apparently not easily deceived. Young Nigel Fortescue seemed to be well received by her for a while, but she eventually sent him packing with a flea in his ear."

"Good Lord. Whatever for? The Fortescues are the very cream of the *ton*, and Nigel cuts a fine enough figure."

"I have it on very good authority that she caught him dallying with one of her chambermaids. A fetching little petticoat, by all accounts."

"The devil you say?" Lampson stroked his chin. "This 'good authority' could be mistaken. Who was it?"

"My butler. Servants know more about what goes on above-stairs than we do ourselves."

"Quite. Then the sordid little tale must be true. Fetching little petticoat, eh?" Lampson chuckled suggestively. "I wonder what became of her?"

"Fortescue has her cozily ensconced in a modest little town house, I believe."

Lampson slapped his thigh. "Good for him. She cost him dearly—it would have been a shame to let her go to waste." He braced his shoulders. "Well, old chap, nothing worth having comes easily. It is time to beard the lioness in her den. Or should I say, ballroom?"

"Just remember how magnificent a place it is," Delville rejoined. "It will help to keep you focused whilst you court our reluctant heiress." He bowed and gestured toward the heavy double doors. "After you, would-be father to the future Earl of Camberly."

Seething with outrage, Althea watched as the two men, seemingly overcome by their own wit, exited the library, laughing like a pair of demented hyenas.

Once alone, Althea's emotions ran the gamut from teeth-clenching anger to wounded sensibilities, ending with the mortifying conclusion that compared to all the birds-of-paradise who at that very moment were most likely flaunting their feathers in the ballroom, she must be the veriest of sparrows.

The exchange between the two gentlemen merely confirmed her worst fears. Not one of her suitors was likely to look beyond her fortune and seek to marry her for herself.

"Even so," she muttered, "I would gladly see the Markham line die out rather than marry such an odious toad. What gives Francis Lampton cause to think he is in any position to assess *my* desirability as a mate?"

Althea rose from her chair and tried in vain to smooth her rumpled dress. Then it occurred to her that the offending gentlemen had not even taken the trouble to extinguish the candles before their departure.

With an exasperated huff, she picked up the discarded decanter of cognac and returned it to the cabinet in which her great-uncle Jean-Claude kept his precious, not-to-be-shared contraband.

Upon closing the cabinet door, her brow knitted into a perplexed frown. The old gentleman might be approaching the ripe old age of seventy, but he was not given to forgetfulness—of a certainty not where his cognac was concerned—yet he had failed to secure it under lock and key.

Althea was about to snuff out the candles when she caught sight of her reflection in a small mirror hanging on the wall above the cabinet. Moving the light to a more advantageous position, she peered thoughtfully into the mirror and ran her hand down her cheek and across the angle of her jaw.

"George Delville is absolutely right. My features *are* completely unworthy of attention. Although how he could have failed to notice my lamentably square jaw…" Althea shook her head while contemplating this point.

Actually, a discerning eye would have noticed that her strong jaw was in perfect symmetry to her well-defined cheekbones and, by way of contrast gave her mouth a rose-petal softness—at least on the rare occasions when she did not press her lips into a grim line. Althea took the responsibilities of running her estates very seriously.

"Eyes like moonstones, hmmm? What could George Delville have possibly meant by that?" She leaned closer to the mirror. "They are shaped well enough, I suppose, but I expect comparing them to moonstones is a polite way of saying they lack color. Oh, well." She gave a philosophic shrug and blew out the candles, pulling a face at the resultant acrid smoke.

The ball not coming to a close until almost daybreak, Althea did not make her way downstairs until noon and found upon inquiring of Jarvis, the butler, that he believed she was the first of the family to rise. In any case, neither the elder Lady Camberly nor the Marquis de Maligny had as yet put in an appearance for breakfast.

This suited her very well, because she was in no mood to exchange pleasantries with her relations. Indeed, where the older Lady Camberly was concerned, Althea was not sure she could maintain even the merest of civilities. Her lady mother's behavior at the ball the previous evening had been outside of outrageous.

With this thought in mind, she decided to forgo breakfast in favor of the serenity of the orangerie. There she settled into a white wicker sofa's plump cushions of flowered chintz, and looked about her. The tropical foliage laden with exotic and sweet-smelling blossoms usually lifted her spirits. But not this morning. She was far too upset over the indignities she had endured in the library at the hands of those insufferable boors, Delville and Lampson.

In spite of her woes, Althea smiled. Revenge was sweet. When Francis Lampson had been presented to her shortly after the ghastly scene in the library, she had received him with the sort of look one usually accords squashed frogs. The hapless young man bowed his way out of the situation, stammering his "ahems" with red-faced confusion.

"I doubt he will present himself on Wednesday."

"To whom do you refer, *chérie?*"

Althea started. She had not heard her uncle enter the orangerie and, until addressed, was unaware that she had spoken out loud. Her heart sank. Now she would be obliged to discuss last night's ball with the old gentleman, and what was worse, also be subjected to his usual dissertation on the inferiority of the English way of life.

"Good morning—good afternoon, rather. The ball went over rather well, do you not agree, Uncle?" Althea was safe in assuming that if she changed the subject, her great-uncle Jean-Claude would neglect to notice that his question had not been answered. He was of an age where he could be distracted if the subject at hand bore no particular significance for him.

"I quite agree. It was an amusing little gathering. Elegant

enough by English standards, I suppose." This remark was accompanied by a pinch-nosed sniff.

An amusing little gathering indeed! The Camberly ball had been the crush of the season. Althea fixed her gaze on a stuffed parrot perched on the lower branches of a mimosa tree. Its lifelike quality attested to the taxidermist's art. In her mind's eye, Althea substituted the rather portly frame of her great-uncle in its stead. She knew the brittle limbs of a mimosa tree could not possibly hold his weight, but this did not lessen her pleasure.

She hoped the lateness of the previous evening's affair had left the Marquis de Maligny too fatigued to dwell long on the past splendors of the French court. With little hope for her wishes coming to fruition, she steeled herself for what was to follow, and did what she always did at such times: her utmost to block out the sound of his voice.

It did not take long for Althea's fertile mind to carry her back to the previous evening's debacle. Of course the ball *had* been a social triumph, a veritable feather in her cap, one might say, but her horrid experience in the library piled upon her mother's mortifying behavior had rendered it the most disagreeable experience of her life.

Well, perhaps not the *most* disagreeable—nothing could top finding that perfidious bounder Nigel Fortescue in the feverish act of raising her chambermaid's skirts. In Althea's own sewing room, no less. If the little jade had not let out such screams of pleasure, they never would have been found out and she, Althea, would have married him and he most likely—nay, most *definitely*—would have carried on his shameful liaison right under her nose!

Suddenly her kinsman's voice impinged upon her consciousness.

"But of course it goes without saying that the ballroom at Versailles is without equal." He punctuated this remark with an expansive gesture.

"I regret that I have not had the opportunity to see it for myself," Althea inserted.

"Did I not tell you that the queen used to single me out for special consideration?"

"I seem to recall such," she responded. *Only on every possible occasion since I was old enough to comprehend.*

"When it came to the dance, *La Belie Reine* declared me to be the most skilled of her courtiers. She would…" His voice trailed off.

After a moment or two of silence, Althea shot him a glance. The marquis was known to nod off at the oddest moments. This was not the case. With eyes unfocused and bedewed with unshed tears, he seemed to be transported to another time and place. No doubt that gilded era when he had been young and handsome, and had danced with a queen.

Althea was jolted into a feeling of profound pity for him. She laid a hand over his and determined that in the future, she would listen when he shared his memories of past glories. After all, they were the things he treasured the most.

He looked startled by her touch, and then a warm smile wreathed his face. "Ah, Althea, my dear, dear, niece. Your kind regard is a great comfort under my present circumstances." He clasped her hand with both of his and gave it a warm squeeze. "I await the day when my beloved chateau, Alençon, is restored to me. Then I shall have the pleasure of returning your hospitality in the grand French manner."

His tone implied that English hospitality did not—indeed, *could* not—measure up to that of the French. In spite of her newfound resolve to be patient and forbearing with her uncle, she was sorely tempted to shake him hard enough to rid him of his complacent belief in the superiority of all things French.

Althea's temporary lack of goodwill quickly passed, to be replaced by another wave of pity for the old gentleman. It was highly unlikely that his dream of returning to his former stature as a great French lord would be realized. What harm was there in allowing him a little grandiosity from time to time?

She thanked him prettily for his kind intentions and then searched for a way to take her leave as graciously as possible. A moment or two later, providence breezed by the window in the form of her mother, her arms laden with a basket filled with a profusion of daffodils.

"Please excuse me, Uncle dear. I wish to speak with Mama before she departs on her social rounds."

Jean-Claude glanced outside in time to catch a carefree wave from Celeste. He returned the greeting with a frown. Althea surmised that on the previous evening, word of Celeste's scandalous behavior had filtered into the salon where the older gentlemen played card games.

"Hmmph. I am thinking that the little *cocotte* is looking far too pleased for her own good," he muttered. "Her tryst with Viscount Ridley last evening must have been *most* fulfilling."

"Uncle! That is highly improper."

"Forgive me, *ma petite*. I must have been thinking out loud. But even so, as head of this family you cannot afford to affect— how do you say?—such missish ways. Your mama must be persuaded to exercise a little discretion. If you are not up to the task, I will undertake to do it for you."

"I am afraid I must decline your kind offer. Mama is not a child to be told what she can, or cannot, do. Besides, I refuse to think the worst of her."

At least, not out loud, and certainly not to another living soul.

"You are forbearing to a fault, Althea. But then, you have always had a kind heart."

Althea raised a brow. "Sir, you surprise me. You are the last person I would take for a puritan, especially coming from the French court. In fact, I find your attitude in this matter most puzzling. Most puzzling indeed."

The marquis pinched her cheek. "When did *you* become so tolerant of the peccadilloes of the *ton, chérie?*"

Althea gave a shrug. "Come now. It is not unusual for widows to, er, enjoy certain freedoms. I know Society does not *condone* such things, but a blind eye is turned. Most of the ladies concerned are still accepted in the highest circles."

"But of course. The English have a certain modicum of sophistication, thank goodness. I have had my share of *belles amies.*"

"Under the circumstance, I find your attitude towards

Mama most forbidding. I thought you loved her."

The marquis ran his fingers through a head of luxuriant white curls. "The love I have for both you and your mama is that of a father. That is why I suffer such distress over the matter. Celeste has never been one to indulge in such excesses. I did not think it to be in her nature. She was a virtuous young creature. Never a breath of scandal." He gestured toward Althea. "In that way you are both alike—at least, until the last year or so. This liaison with such a rake degrades her. Your *chère* mama should find a worthier gentleman to love. One of infinite kindness and discretion—non?"

"Of course I would agree. But I refuse to believe Mama was guilty last night of anything more than a harmless stroll in the garden."

"But of course, my child. A wise and proper decision, to be sure." The distance in his tone belied his response. "Now if you will excuse me, I believe I am ready for my breakfast"

He strode from her presence with the vigor of a much younger man. In spite of a thickening waistline, he carried himself with a natural grace. It occurred to Althea that it was well within the bounds of possibility that the last queen of France had indeed found him to be a *most* pleasing dance partner.

Althea hoped it was enough to sustain him during his subsequent exile, but had her doubts. While musing on the subject, she happened to glance outside once more. Celeste was sitting on a bench, her face buried in the bouquet of daffodils.

She chose that moment to raise her head and blow a kiss in Althea's direction. Althea was neither touched nor amused by the show of affection. Mama had to be aware that today, tongues in drawing rooms all over Town were most likely wagging over her dalliance in the garden with the dashing Marcus Ridley.

"I must convince Mama that it is in her best interest to return to the country as soon as possible," Althea murmured as she rose from her seat. She started for the door leading to the garden, then stood stock-still and let out a groan. "I am afraid that should be *our* best interest. The *ton* must also find *my* inability to keep suitors from exploring beneath the petticoats of my chambermaids highly diverti—"

She stopped short, realizing that an onlooker might think she was engaged in a heartfelt conversation with the stuffed parrot. This convinced Althea that it was time to depart the social round of London in favor of the soothing calm of Camberly Hall. To this end, she joined her mother in the garden.

Chapter 2

Althea approached her mother, fully expecting her to balk at the idea of leaving London before the Season had ended.

"I intend to leave for Camberly no later than Tuesday," she said. "I would dearly love for you to accompany me."

"But of course, darling."

"I know you adore London, but I would deem it a favor if you could tear yourself away. I will do my best to make it up to you." Althea's was the rapid delivery of one who held out little hope for having her wishes realized.

Celeste tapped her on the shoulder with one of her daffodils. "My darling little cabbage, it is as I thought. You seldom listen to a word I say. I said I would accompany you."

Althea could not believe how easy it had been. She searched her mother's expression to make sure she was not teasing. Celeste's brilliant green eyes were filled with deep-to-the-bone sincerity. This gave Althea a feeling of unease that she immediately dismissed on realizing that the tip of Celeste's nose was coated with the yellow pollen of daffodils. How could anyone who looked so guileless possibly be up to something, and yellow-tipped nose notwithstanding, yet manage to look so extravagandy beautiful in the unforgiving brightness of a springtime sun?

Although vaguely aware that her reasoning did not exactly weigh heavily on the side of logic, Althea chose to dismiss the subject from her mind and hastened indoors to inform both of their abigails of their impending return to the Sussex countryside.

After a week at Camberly Hall, Althea found that she was filled with a strange restlessness. This feeling was alien to her and she wondered as to the cause. Could it possibly be due to the unsettling experience of eavesdropping in the library the night of the ball? She had known immediately that it had been a mistake—or had it? After all, it had firmed her resolve not to be taken in by would-be title seekers and fortune hunters.

It took another week for Althea to realize that this was not the case. This occurred when she happened to be passing the ballroom, and as was her wont, stopped to admire the magnificent painted ceiling; through the door, she espied her mother engaged in a graceful waltz in the arms of an imaginary partner.

It hit her like a bolt of lightning. The source of her disquietude was a need for the sort of romance that seemed to befall her mother by right of being. Was it so wrong to want a man to regard her with the same ardor the elder Lady Camberly seemed to engender so effortlessly?

She hurried past the ballroom door and happened to glance at her reflection in a huge looking glass strategically placed for such a purpose. *George Delville is right—I do look like a very prim governess.* She wondered why it had taken the careless words of a Corinthian dandy for her to see what was so painfully evident to others.

Althea pulled a strand of her dark-blond hair out of her bun and it immediately sprang into a curl, curving into the hollow of her cheek. "Such foolishness," she muttered. Not realizing how the effect had softened her features, she pulled the tendril back within the confines of a side-comb.

She turned away from her offending image to see her mother staring at her, a thoughtful expression on her face.

"You should consider the change, darling. It is most becoming."

Althea felt her cheeks flame. How pathetic she must seem. It would take more than a curl or two to make her looks even passable, much less becoming. Obviously, Mama was allowing mother-love to color her judgment.

She gave her head an impatient toss. "I like my hair the way it is. I do not care to sit around all morning while Lizzie pulls it this way and that."

Celeste smiled. "How different we are. I sometimes wonder

if you are a changeling."

Althea stiffened. "I am sorry to be such a disappointment to you, Mama."

Celeste shook her head. "Never think that I could not ask for a better daughter. You always consider the welfare of the rest of us before your own. I know Uncle Jean-Claude can be a pompous bore and your Cousin Philippe is not much better."

"But Cousin Philippe goes to Bedfordshire to visit his maternal grandparents quite frequently. Besides, he is an absolute lamb. He causes no trouble whatsoever."

"*Exactement!* Poor Philippe is twenty-one years old and has yet to defy his grandfather."

Althea was puzzled. "And you find this distressing?"

"But of course. A boy cannot become a man until he develops a backbone. Such a one cannot help but become a burden to all concerned." Celeste gave a wry smile. "And then you have me with whom to contend."

Althea was tempted to respond to this remark. If she could convince her mother to exercise more discretion in the conducting of her personal affairs, perhaps she, Althea, would be able to sleep more soundly at night. Instead, she said, "Please do not refine on the matter, darling. We are a very small family and I would be terribly lonely if any of you were to pack your bags and decide to live in the dower house."

This sentiment earned Althea a pat on the cheek. "Very prettily put, *ma petite*, but if you had the courage to be beautiful, a handsome gentleman would fall madly in love with you and in no time at all you would have this enormous edifice absolutely crawling with children."

"*Mama!*"

Celeste rolled her eyes. "*Mon Dieu!* Is there no joy in you? You will find that an ability to laugh at oneself makes life run a lot more smoothly."

"I am sorry, Mama, but my experiences of late give more cause for tears than laughter."

Celeste's eyes grew moist and she enfolded Althea in a quick embrace. "Ah, yes. Nigel Fortescue. One day you will be glad you sent him packing. The *cochon* is not fit to breathe the same air as you."

Althea giggled. "You express yourself beautifully, Mama. Nigel is indeed a pig, but I was referring to another distressing incident."

Celeste's face filled with concern. "Oh? Kindly elucidate."

Althea went on to explain her experience in the library, leaving out none of the humiliating details save those that bore reference to Celeste's escapade.

"Pah! Pigs, pigs, pigs. One would expect such behavior of any spawn of Baron Lampton's, but in George's case, I feel you have been utterly betrayed. We all have. You have been playmates since you were both in leading strings."

"I know. That was the unkindest cut of all. George has received his last invitation from me, but I shall not lend him the importance of an outright snub. A certain coolness will do. I am sure that after a while he will begin to fret over the lack of a social life."

A Gallic chuckle gurgled from the back of Celeste's throat. *'Mais oui.* The perfect revenge. Your affairs are the only contact George has to the upper stratum of society—the Lamptons hardly count since they seldom go to town, thank goodness. Without your *cachet,* I doubt George will cut such a fine figure."

Althea frowned. "You do not think I am being too harsh on poor George?"

Celeste threw up her hands. *'Poor* George, is it now? Althea darling, I wash my hands of the whole affair. Do as you think fit."

As I think fit. I had thought my own corner of the world and everyone in it fitted quite nicely into cozy little slots over which I had perfect control. What a fool I turned out to be!

Celeste inspected her reflection in the mirror, rearranged an unruly curl, and gave Althea a reassuring smile. "Do not give the matter another thought, darling. Such people do not deserve the effort it requires."

It occurred to Althea that perhaps it was this philosophy that enabled her mother to keep the wrinkles at bay.

"I am going into the village this afternoon," Celeste

continued. "I have been told that Hansford's has a new supply of silks and muslins in stock. I wish you would accompany me. It would not hurt you to have some new dresses for summer. We could have Madame Zizette come and make them up for us. I am sure she would welcome a month or two away from the city."

Althea gave a dry laugh. "I suppose she would. She made herself so welcome last summer, she spent an extra week letting out the seams of her own dresses before returning to London."

"So you will come with me today?"

Althea nodded. "I think the excursion might do me some good."

Celeste rewarded her with a beaming smile.

Celeste decided that they should make the trip to Camberly Village without any servants tagging along.

"We might wish to talk."

Celeste handled horses as well as any man and loved to drive a handsome equipage, but Althea insisted they make the trip in the pony-and-trap. She found her mother's bold way with anything more powerful far too unsettling.

Hansford's was situated on the esplanade facing the ocean. It was a handsome-looking establishment for a village the size of Camberly. Ladies came from as far away as Brighton, a good six miles, to purchase the fine materials and special trims for which the shop was noted.

It was rumored that Hansford's ample supply of goods was due to trading with smugglers who ran the French blockade. As long as the local authorities did not look into the matter, Mr. Hansford's customers considered the rumors to be just that, and continued to give him their patronage.

It was a beautiful day to be by the ocean. For a change, there were few clouds in the sky and the sunlight danced on the waves in a very delightful fashion. Althea felt most exhilarated— too much so, as the thought of spending even a moment in Hansford's musty shop became intolerable.

When their pony-and-trap approached the pier, Althea

put a hand on Celeste's elbow and called out, "Please stop here, Mama."

Celeste complied, then looked about her, taking care to give the pier extra careful scrutiny. "The place is deserted. Why are we stopping?"

Althea gave her a beseeching look. "Forgive me, Mama. I cannot stand the thought of being cooped up in Hansford's on such a glorious day. It is so unusual for April. I should like to take a turn on the pier while you make your purchases."

Celeste gave a little pout. "Althea, it is not well of you. It spoils all our plans for having Madame Zizette come to Camberly. It hardly pays to have her here for my few things."

Althea refrained from mentioning that her mother's purchases seldom amounted to a "few things." Fortunately, the late earl had left his widow with a very generous allowance and it mattered not that she spent twice as much money on her clothes as did the present Countess of Camberly.

Althea was surprised by her own response to her mother's objections. "You pick out some materials for me, Mama. I am probably in need of a couple of new dresses to wear for evening, perhaps one or two for mornings. You know the sort of thing I like. I shall rely entirely on your discretion."

As the pony-and-trap continued its journey along the esplanade, Althea groaned in dismay. "What was I thinking?" she muttered. "Mama does not possess one shred of discretion—at least, not of late. I suppose she is one of those ladies who goes a little off balance with the encroaching years."

Althea climbed down the stone steps leading to the long, wooden pier. She had traversed about a quarter of the length of the structure when a breeze began to whip about, causing her skirts to flap like sheets drying on a clothesline. A most undignified turn of events, but fortunately, the pier was devoid of onlookers. In the distance she saw a small dory departing from what she presumed was a merchant vessel.

The wind picked up a notch and Althea fastened the frogging on her coat, a drab but serviceable garment about the same shade of brown as the donkeys one could hire farther down the beach for children to ride.

Bending forward to brace against what was now a decidedly forceful wind, Althea gritted her teeth and doggedly continued her walk. At this point she admitted to herself that an afternoon spent fingering silks in Mr. Hansford's emporium sounded a great deal more attractive than battling the elements on the pier.

With this thought in mind, Althea decided to retrace her steps. It made far more sense to walk the half-mile or so to the shop than to stay on the pier to be buffeted by what had turned into a most unpleasant breeze. Experience told her that her mother would take the better part of an hour making her purchases before giving a thought to returning to pick her up.

As she turned, she looked up to see that the dory was pushing off from the pier steps with only one passenger aboard. To her consternation, she saw him leaning against the pier rail staring at her, a quizzical look on his face.

Miserably aware that the wind molded her skirts to her bottom in a most scandalous manner, Althea broke into an unladylike run. To her mortification, she tripped over an uneven plank and went sprawling. The breath knocked out of her, she just lay there, railing at her own stupidity. The damage to her pride hurt far more than the stinging pain she felt on her hands and knees.

While she struggled to stand up, a strong pair of hands grasped her by the elbows and drew her to her feet. The man put a steadying hand on her shoulder, and she noticed that beneath a windblown mop of light brown curls, his clear, gray eyes were filled with concern.

On closer inspection she realized his clothes were of a better quality and far cleaner than those of an ordinary seafarer, and assumed that he was a junior officer or a passenger on board the vessel, which would account for his having been deposited on the pier. However, this did not excuse his impertinence. How dare he put his hands on a lady.

"I trust you did not hurt yourself, miss?"

He spoke in a softer version of the local accent, the sound less exaggerated, his words crisper and more precise. Althea wondered if he had been educated at a dame school, or perhaps by a neighboring parson.

She brushed his hand from her shoulder. "Thank you, no."

As if unaware of the cold reception he had received, he accorded her a brilliant smile.

Up to that point, Althea had assessed his looks as quite nondescript, that is, if one discounted those romantic-looking curls. But his smile had the effect of displaying a flash of even, white teeth and brought about a most disconcerting dimpling of his cheeks.

Althea suffered a tiny jolt in the pit of her stomach and struggled to catch her breath.

"You look awfully pale, miss. I think you should sit down until you feel better."

Without waiting for a reply, he took her arm and led her to a bench. Althea complied without a murmur. The man then removed his jacket and placed it around her shoulders and sat down beside her.

"Really," she remonstrated, "this is quite unnecessary."

"I cannot agree. I rather think I should see you home. Where do you live?"

See her home, indeed. The man overstepped himself. Althea pointed to a large house on the esplanade. It belonged to a family named Swann. The Swanns had five lively boys whom Althea invited to picnics by the river at Camberly Hall from time to time.

"I take it you are the governess?"

Althea fought back the urge to wince. She looked down at her drab coat, vowing to give it to her abigail. As George had so succinctly stated, one would not take her for a lady of title and great fortune.

"I fit the mold, plain and nondescript, would you not agree?"

He gave her a sharp look. "No, I would not. I rather suspect you go out of your way not to bring attention upon yourself, but with your extraordinary eyes and your marvelous bone structure, you have a beauty that transcends both time and fashion."

Althea stiffened. The presumptuous fellow! Such patronizing flattery would not be welcomed if it came from the lips of a gentleman of the *ton*, much less from one who was obviously a social inferior. She gave him what she hoped was a forbidding look.

"Sir, your outrageous remarks were neither sought nor welcomed. Such a tarradiddle does not recommend you."

To add weight to her disapproval, she rose from the bench, removed his jacket from her shoulders, and handed it to him.

He stood up to receive it. His lips parted momentarily as if to voice protest, but he evidently thought better of it and gave Althea a rueful smile instead.

"Please accept my apologies, miss. My words were most untoward, I grant you, but I stand by their veracity."

"Perhaps. But it would be most improper for me to stay and continue this conversation. I bid you good day, sir."

This time, Althea took great pains not to trip while making her departure. When she reached the end of the pier, she turned around and discovered he was standing exactly where she had left him, resolutely staring in her direction.

With a sigh of resignation, Althea crossed the road and made her way to the Swann residence. Before raising the door-knocker, she looked over her shoulder. It was, as she feared. The man had not budged an inch.

It was not until Mary Swann dispatched a footman to Hansford's to inform the older Lady Camberly of the whereabouts of her daughter that it dawned on Althea that she did not even know the impudent stranger's name.

Chapter 3

John Ridley watched the young woman retrace her steps along the pier, highly intrigued by the imperious manner of her bearing.

She is angry enough to have my guts for garters. I cannot imagine what prompted me to say them, but who would have thought a few complimentary words would transform the little mouse into a raging tiger? I must remember to be more circumspect in the future.

It occurred to John that a further encounter with the governess was hardly likely. He was surprised at the sense of loss this thought seemed to invoke.

As soon as he saw that she was safely admitted into the large white house, he also left the pier and, turning right, proceeded to walk the length of the esplanade.

He noticed a pony-and-trap tethered to a hitching post outside of Hansford's and glanced through the window. A lady with fiery red curls peeking below the brim of a very becoming ivory colored bonnet held a swathe of yellow silk to her cheek. She caught his glance and with a slight smile, turned her back on him.

John grinned. It occurred to him one was scarcely likely to find *that* particular beauty wearing brown, at least not the drab, nondescript shade favored by the governess who had so hastily beat a retreat into the large white house across from the pier.

He took three more steps and stopped short. Why in thunder did the governess constantly come to mind? Then it dawned on him that she had never really left, but rather flitted in and out of his consciousness like a persistent gnat.

With an impatient shrug, he strode past Hansford's and towards his destination, an inn a hundred yards farther down the road. A sign above the door bearing the legend The Boar's

Head, with the appropriate tusked head painted on it, creaked back and forth in the wind.

The innkeeper had once told John that the inn dated back to the reign of Henry VIII, a respite for travelers thirty years before his daughter Elizabeth bestowed the earldom of Camberly upon Walter Markham. "A handsome devil, by all accounts," the publican had added. The esplanade was a more recent addition to Camberly.

Once inside, John scanned the room to find it was empty. Marcus was supposed to have met him there five minutes ago. It was highly unlikely that his brother would not allow him a few minutes' grace; therefore, he concluded, Marcus must be late.

John felt a rising irritation. True, he was also late, but in his view, he was putting up with all the discomfort their arrangement afforded, and as far as *he* was concerned, Marcus could at least be on time once in a while.

There was nothing for it but to sit down and wait for him. At least, he thought, they have excellent ale here.

He chose a table by the window. The small bull's-eye panes of glass obscured the identities of those who did so from any who chanced to pass by.

Without being asked, a serving girl brought him a tankard of ale. She was a winsome young thing, pleasingly plump with dark drown curls framing rosy cheeks and sparkling brown eyes.

John smiled at her. "Thank you, Betsy."

Betsy responded with a slight bob. "Would you like something to eat, sir? Cook has made a very tasty lamb stew."

John shook his head. "Not today. Some bread and cheese would be more to my liking, thank you."

He had sampled "Cook's" lamb stew on a previous occasion. Its flavor had owed more to a sheep of mature years than any lamb he had ever tasted. He had no desire to repeat the experience.

Betsy bobbed once more and left to do his bidding, her hips swaying a good deal more than was necessary to get her to the kitchen. John was the only patron in the room, although he could hear the boisterous laughter of local fishermen in the adjoining taproom. Her performance had to be for his benefit.

John shook his head. In spite of a ripe figure, Betsy's features proclaimed her to be no more than fourteen at most. He dreaded to think what kind of a future she was choosing for herself. Girls of that age could be so vulnerable, and unfortunately, such behavior was not confined to the lower classes.

He recalled the lovesick young chit of the same age who had somehow managed to secrete herself in his brother Marcus's chambers the previous summer. Upon ascertaining that the viscount had no intention of entering into a forced marriage with their wayward offspring, her parents abruptly ceased their cries of outrage and quickly bundled her into their carriage and took their leave.

According to Marcus, the girl's parents managed to keep the incident a secret, for not a breath of scandal circulated among the *ton*. The following year, at the tender age of fifteen and without the benefit of a "come-out," the girl was married off to a country squire. "Her parents are undoubtedly relieved to be rid of such a handful," Marcus had added.

John's life had taken a far different turn. While his brother Marcus had been dodging traps set for him by every predatory lady of the *ton,* on their own behalf or that of their daughters, he had spent the three years in Jamaica, diligently managing Marydene, the family's sugar plantation.

It was there that he had met and fallen in love with Belinda Vickery, a young lady visiting her uncle on the adjoining plantation. John was surprised to notice that the memory of Belinda, the turquoise shallows of the Caribbean echoing the extraordinary color of her eyes and the sun transforming her hair to a golden fire, did not seem to evoke as sharp a pain as it once had. Although he doubted he would ever forget her final words when she had broken off their betrothal.

"Of course I love you, darling, but it just will not do. You should have made it *clear* that Marydene is not yours." She punctuated the following words with what he used to think was an adorable little moue. "After all, you cannot expect me to scrape by on the expectations of a second son."

He had been so shocked by the bluntness of her delivery and the calculating coldness that had inspired it that he omitted to tell her that he was heir to a considerable fortune from a maternal aunt.

A week later, Belinda became engaged to a Mr. Ralph Portman, a houseguest of her uncle's whose lack of pedigree, apparently, was amply compensated by the considerable size of his fortune. For some reason, this news only filled John with profound pity for the prospective groom.

John was sensible enough to realize that he had not fallen in love with the real Belinda—indeed, he had found nothing desirable about the person lurking behind the pretty facade. Nevertheless, the revelation had been a nasty shock and he doubted he would trust a member of the fair sex ever again.

Overnight, the island he deemed to be a paradise on earth struck him as being more like a prison. One from which he could not wait to escape. Six months later he turned over the management of Marydene to a competent man of impeccable reputation and returned to England to what he hoped would be the comforting bosom of his family.

John drained his tankard of the final drop of ale and slammed it down on the table and growled under his breath, "I must have been mad to harbor such illusions."

That had been over a year ago and without so much as a commiserating word, Marcus had said, "Good. Now you are home you can help me, but most importantly, you can help your country."

At the time John had considered it the perfect solution to deal with what he perceived to be the aimlessness and loneliness that had taken over his life, so before he could catch his breath he agreed to a role that encompassed becoming both a spy and a fomenter of unrest against the French.

It did not take him long to discover that the new path he had chosen for himself only compounded his problems. He found out what it was like to be cut off from the comforts of life as the son of the Earl of Fairfax and consigned to the discomfort of plying the channel between England and France carrying information to both shores. The cramped quarters he was given in the small boat did nothing to improve his humor.

He found his loss of social status the greater indignity. Even the second son of an earl is used to being treated with deference. In the guise of a mariner of questionable rank on a boat of no great consequence, he was lucky to enjoy the respect of a tavern wench, much less his equals. Even the little governess had treated him like some creature a cat had left on the doorstep.

"There I go again," he muttered. "Will she never leave my mind? It's like jiggling a loose tooth."

Realizing he was talking out loud, he snapped his mouth closed, thinking that his predicament was caused by the loneliness of the task he had chosen. He had pointed out to Marcus that his was the more onerous position. The spy business had not changed Marcus's life one whit, except, perhaps, to color it with a little excitement.

Marcus had put a sympathetic arm around his shoulder. "I realize that old chap. I would give my right arm to trade places with you, but with you being out of the country for so long, and being such a recluse, an occasional person might run into you and see a resemblance to our family. However, with the awful cut of that sailor's garb you are forced to wear, they will hardly think it *is* you. At worst you will probably be taken for a by-blow of father's."

"I say," John remonstrated, "that is a bit thick."

"Nonsense." Marcus gave a dismissive shrug. "See it all the time. Many a village is dotted with the indiscretions of its local gentry."

John's reverie was interrupted by the return of Betsy with his platter of cheese and bread, which was accompanied by a crock of butter, another tankard of ale, and a coy fluttering of eyelashes.

"Will that be all, sir?"

He found the sultry manner in which she posed the question somewhat disconcerting. "For the time being," he responded, taking care to make his tone as impersonal as possible.

Betsy's flouncing exit made it perfectly clear that his

snub had been duly noted and resented. John shook his head, slathered some butter on a crusty chunk of bread, then broke off a piece of the local cheese from the generous wedge he had been given. He knew from past experience that it had a nutlike flavor blended with a sharp pungency that was sheer bliss to the palate and lost no time in tucking in to it.

After savoring the last crumb, he settled back to enjoy his ale. It wasn't until his tankard was half empty that it occurred to him that by now, his brother was not only outrageously late, but it was doubtful he would show up at all. That meant a moonlight liaison with his go-between.

"Damned inconvenient," he muttered. "I had hoped to leave for Calais with the evening tide."

John gave his brother another half-hour, then paid for his meal and left the inn. He did not retrace his steps but turned left and continued to walk until the buildings came to an abrupt end.

Here, John veered onto a dirt lane leading to a cluster of fishermen's cottages situated on the beach. He approached them with a determined stride, not stopping until he had reached one which was set apart from the others.

He stopped to inspect a small dory beached out front, then entered the cottage, the humblest pile in a row of five. All the houses were constructed of stones the local people gathered on the beach at the mouth of the River Camber.

Presently, a plume of smoke curled out of the chimney stack, indicating that the man the local fishermen knew as John Soames intended to stay for a while.

It was as Althea had supposed. On opening her packages from Hansford's, she discovered that her mother had chosen far different materials for her dresses than she would have.

She fingered a dotted muslin in a pale green meant for a morning dress, then held up the yards of beautiful lace intended for its trim. *Mother is an extravagant creature,* she thought, then gasped at the fine shot silk she discovered next. This was an admixture of pale green and lavender that seemed to dance in the light streaming in from her bedroom window.

Yesterday she would have rejected such colors as "too unserviceable," but that was before she had met an outspoken young seafarer who, having mistaken her for a governess, had yet found something to admire in her.

There were several other lengths of material of diverse color and texture. Twice as many as she had requested. Althea held each in turn to her face before the mirror, fascinated how every one seemed to enhance her delicate coloring—especially the green-and-lavender silk.

Althea draped it around her shoulders and studied the results once more, marveling at how the colors seemed to work magic on the green of her eyes—until self-doubt colored her judgment. The sparkle left her eyes and she discarded the shimmering material in a ruck on top of the rest of the materials covering her counterpane like a spring flowerbed.

"What was Mama thinking?" she murmured.

She walked over to her bedroom window, a tall, square-paned opening taking up the better part of a wall, and stared pensively at the garden below. Her bedroom faced the rear of the house, overlooking a pleasant garden laid out with flowerbeds and tree-lined paths. A large pond filled with carp and water lilies and shaded by a graceful weeping willow reminded Althea of the willow pattern on the blue-and-white china used in the morning room at breakfast time. In the distance, flashes of the River Camber gleamed through the trees growing along the riverbank.

Althea usually found solace, and even delight, in this vista, depending on her mood; but now, her gaze was unseeing, her shoulders slumped. She was still standing there, silhouetted against the glow of twilight, when Lizzie came to help her dress for dinner.

Chapter 4

Althea remained pensive during dinner, responding to her mother's efforts to be sociable with little more than a "yes" or a "no." She was too preoccupied with thoughts of her encounter with the young man that afternoon. She smiled briefly, recalling the compliment he paid her, then was quick to remind herself that he had also mistaken her for a governess.

On being asked by her mother if the dress lengths she had chosen were to her liking, Althea had replied, "They are all very beautiful. It was kind of you to take the trouble, Mama."

Althea could not summon the energy to inform her that she had no intention of having dresses made up in any of her choices. Tomorrow would be soon enough. She expected to be forgiven when her mother learned that not only would she be making her a gift of the lovely materials, but also intended to pay Madame Zizette to make them up for her.

While the thought was still fresh in her mind, she sent a rider to London to inform the dressmaker that her services were required at Camberly Hall.

Later, not wishing to engage in the exchange of after-dinner *on dits* or the playing of cards, Althea decided to forgo the ritual of retiring to the withdrawing room. She intended to use a headache as the reason for depriving her mother of their nightly game of cards. To her surprise, it was her mother who brought up the subject.

With catlike grace, the older Lady Camberly arched her back and gave Althea a rueful smile. "Please forgive me if I do not keep you company, *ma petite*, but this has been a most exhausting day. I can scarcely keep my eyes open."

Althea nodded. "I have to agree, Mama. I should not have

taken that walk on the pier—the strong breeze made it very difficult. I, for one, am only too ready to retire."

Once in her room, Althea endured the ministrations of her efficient abigail, even meekly submitting to laying her head on her pillow a full hour before her normal bedtime. Once Lizzie had departed her chamber, Althea bolted out of her bed and proceeded to pace the floor.

When the fire in the hearth turned to embers, the resulting chill convinced her to return to the comfort of her bedcovers. She tried to think of cheerful things: lambs gamboling in the meadows in the early spring; the carp gliding beneath the lily pads in the garden pond. But the more unsettling thoughts would not be held at bay, and sleep eluded her.

She constantly rehashed her encounter with the young man who had come to her aid on the pier that afternoon. She vividly recalled how the sunlight had imbued his crisp, brown curls with a fiery nimbus, rather like some paintings she had seen of celestial visitors.

The mere fact that she was even capable of such thoughts caused Althea deep distress. She was angry with herself for giving in to what she considered to be a ridiculous fancy. There had been nothing angelic in the feelings his smile had stirred within her.

Then there was the matter of his voice. It had been soft yet deep, and as disturbing as a caress. What was it he had said to her? Ah, yes. His words resonated in her head. Words that sent her heart soaring. Words that spoke of her beauty transcending time and fashion. Words she would carry in her heart to hold the hurt at bay.

Beauty I did not go out of my way to bring attention to. How does one go about bringing attention to a beauty that is so well hidden? I swear I cannot find a trace of it. In any case, it is a very odd thing to say. How can one choose to be beautiful? Either one is, or one is not. That is that, cut and dried. The man is definitely a rascal.

Althea sat up. *But do not his words echo those which Mama had to say on the subject? "If you had the courage to be beautiful, a handsome gentleman would fall in love with you." I am thinking that Mama and the young man are both mad, each in their own way.*

The words thundered over and over in her head. *If you had the courage,* became interchangeable with, *I suspect you do not go out of your way.*

Althea clutched her ears. "Go away. I am not a coward. And neither would primping and preening make of me a heroine."

In spite of her protest, Althea decided that her mother would not be receiving the gift of extra dress lengths after all. Althea did not think for a moment that improving her sense of style would miraculously turn her into a diamond of the first water, but saw no reason why a countess of great fortune should give anyone reason to mistake her for a lowly governess.

With this resolve, Althea lay down once more and in the hope of getting a good night's sleep, pulled the covers over her head. Five minutes later, she sat up once more, positive that sleep eluded her because she had omitted to take her evening constitutional around the grounds before dinner.

It took another five minutes to decide that there was no earthly reason not to take her walk there and then. After all, the garden was illuminated by the brilliance of a full moon.

Holding on to this thought, she abandoned her bed and put on some stockings and shoes, and not wishing to struggle with the fastenings of a dress, put on a fur-lined cloak over her nightrail. Then, bracing her shoulders, she opened her chamber door and went downstairs to her sewing room whence she gained entry to the garden through a French door.

She walked across the lawn, her thoughts quieting as she beheld the splendor of the night sky. Myriad stars sprinkling the dark vault of the sky bespoke a celestial grandeur.

Althea's own problems paled to insignificance when held up to a larger scheme and gradually melted away like snow in a spring thaw. Lifted of their burden, she felt an incredible lightness of being that filled her with a joyous urge to rip off her clothes and dance in the moonlight.

She immediately dismissed this notion as sheer madness, probably brought on by the fullness of the moon. Besides, she reasoned, shocked by her indelicate thoughts, the nip of frost in the air would guarantee such impropriety would be met with a well-deserved demise by lung fever.

Her reverie was interrupted by the sound of footsteps crunching along a gravel path. Not wishing to risk discovery in such a scandalous state of undress, especially by one of the servants, she moved into the shadows of the shrubbery.

To her surprise, the intruder proved to be her own mother, her face as pale as alabaster in the moonlight. Althea's first instinct was to join her, but there was something in the determination of her step and resolution of her expression which caused Althea to doubt that her company would be welcomed.

Althea watched her mother's progress, fully expecting her to turn at the fork leading to the lily pond; instead, she continued to walk straight ahead in the direction of the riverbank.

"What can possess Mama?" Althea mused under her breath. "The riverbank is overgrown with nettles and brambles. It is not at all the sort of place I would expect her to choose for a stroll, by day or night."

She stood shivering in the shadows for about half an hour before her mother reentered the hall. She went through the same French door that Althea had used. Althea followed soon after, glad to get back to the warmth of her bed. However, the walk in the garden notwithstanding, it was dawn before she finally drifted off to sleep, and she did not rise until noon.

Upon going down to breakfast, she was relieved to find that her mother had yet to put in an appearance. She felt guilty for having spied on her and did not wish to look her in the eye.

When she was a little girl, her mother always seemed to know when she had done something wrong and Althea did not want to take the chance that she still had that power. She ate her porridge and stewed apples, thankful to be alone.

After breakfast she exchanged the muslin dress she had worn down to breakfast for a costume fashioned of warm merino wool in a dark green to wear for her morning walk. Following the military style, an influence of the war against Napoleon, it was embellished with epaulettes of black cording and was the most stylish ensemble Althea owned. Unfortunately, the outfit did nothing to enhance her delicate coloring.

As Althea stared into her mirror, watching Lizzy fasten the black frogging, she realized this.

"Lizzie, I look absolutely ghastly in these clothes. Look how awful this green looks on me and how grotesque these exaggerated epaulettes are. I look deformed."

"Yes, madam."

"*Yes, madam*? Is that all you have to say? Lizzie, why did you not say something? I could not look more hideous if I tried."

"It was not my place to say anything, now was it?"

Althea patted her shoulder. "No, Lizzie, I suppose not."

She went downstairs, her head spinning with turmoil, just as her mother was leaving her room. Althea presumed she was on her way to partake of a belated breakfast. She noted that her mother's eyes were free of the shadows that hers had acquired from too little sleep.

Life seems not to touch Mama in any way. Perhaps she is impervious to the vicissitudes that beset the rest of us.

She took a deep breath, deciding to broach her mother about her midnight stroll. "Good morning, Mama. I see you look well in spite of an interrupted sleep."

In response, the older Lady Camberly merely raised a brow.

This came as no surprise to Althea, who was familiar with her mother's habit of skirting unpleasant subjects rather than facing them head-on.

Althea took another deep breath. "I saw you roaming about the gardens last evening. It was late, and quite chilly, so naturally I was concerned about your well-being."

"Were you?" Her words crackled with frost.

The dowager stiffened her back and seeming to grow another inch, towered over her daughter. Althea's first instinct was to back away, but she steeled her resolve and took up the gauntlet.

"Naturally. Especially since you were so tired earlier on. I hope I did nothing to upset you."

Her mother patted her shoulder. "Please do not fuss over me, darling. I am not a child, answerable for my every action."

She broke off for a moment, then added, "How did you come to see me? As I recall, you also claimed to be tired and could not wait to get to bed."

Althea nodded. "I was, but for some reason could not settle down, so I decided to take a walk and that is when I happened to see you."

Celeste responded with a tight little smile. "It would have become you better to have joined me in my walk, rather than to take it upon yourself to subject me to this distasteful interrogation."

Althea bowed slightly. "You are quite right, of course. I did not mean to intrude upon your privacy—I worry too much, I suppose. It really would set my mind at rest if you were to confine such walks to the grounds rather than venture by the river. What if you were to trip over a tree root and fall into the estuary? You could be swept out to sea."

"I rather expect you would."

"Hmm?"

"Prefer that I confine my walks to the grounds."

Althea heaved a sigh of relief. "Then you agree?"

"Of course not, darling." Her tone was incredulous. "Why should I become a prisoner of your morbid fancies?"

Althea pursued the subject no further. How could she? Her clever mother had seen to it that she would be made to feel both unreasonable and foolish.

After that skirmish, both women descended the broad staircase in silence and, on reaching the front hall, exchanged self-conscious smiles before going their separate ways.

Althea returned to the garden to inspect the path her mother had taken the previous night, hoping to find a clue, however slight, that would explain the reason for her midnight jaunt. She did not believe for a moment that her frivolous parent would subject herself to the rigors of a frosty night for the sheer pleasure of the doing.

She found her answer on the bridle path, a narrow lane of mud threading along the riverbank through a jumble of brambles and nettles. There, dainty footprints mingled with those of decidedly masculine proportions.

Further inspection revealed that the man had arrived for their tryst—Althea could think of no other name for such a clandestine meeting—in a small boat. The evidence was all too painfully clear by the scorings on the riverbank where its prow had been pulled out of the water. A wooden peg driven into the weeds and evidently used as a mooring device made Althea think it was not a one-time meeting. She felt her heart lurch.

"Oh, no," she groaned. "For Mama to subject herself to all this inconvenience could only signify that she has fallen in love with an irresistible bounder. One she is ashamed to acknowledge, or even worse, one whose social inferiority precludes her from doing so."

Althea did not wish to believe such a thing of her mother, but it would certainly explain why she had so readily acquiesced to returning to Camberly Hall before the London Season was over.

Feeling thoroughly ignoble at entertaining such suspicions regarding her mother, Althea discarded this supposition and instead grasped at the idea that in the ever-eager quest for ribbons and laces, her mother could be trafficking with a smuggler.

"Yes!" Althea exclaimed. "That must be it. Mama would do so in the blink of an eye for even the tiniest scrap of Alençon lace."

Her relief was fleeting. "What am I thinking? If such were the case, she would be risking far more than a broken heart. She could get her throat cut."

Althea decided she was duty bound to keep a close watch over her.

"It is for Mama's own good."

She doubted such a sentiment on her part would evoke any gratitude in her mother's bosom. By and large, the lady was a lighthearted creature, but cold shivers went down Althea's spine at the possibility of her finding out she was being spied upon.

The general assumption is that a person with ginger hair is inclined to be a trifle hot-tempered. The elder Lady Camberly did not fit into this category. If provoked, *her* ire reached heights of Olympic proportions, giving the very gods good reason to run and hide.

A month passed by, during which Madame Zizette and two of her seamstresses diligently applied themselves to the task of transforming the lengths of material purchased at Hansford's into attractive wearing apparel for her clients.

Even though fearful of the outcome, Althea gave her mother full rein when it came to picking out styles from the pattern books Madame Zizette had brought with her. Once she saw how the clothes transformed her appearance, Althea did not regret her decision.

She stood before a pier glass and ran her hands down an evening dress of white silk with a contrasting heart-shaped bodice in a color her mother identified as willow green. Althea dared to hope it was as becoming as she thought.

"It is a new shade, darling. Mark my words, by next summer *everyone will* be wearing it in one form or another, while *you,* on the other hand, will be setting the style in yet another direction. You shall be the despair of all the would-be fashionables, I promise you."

"Oh, dear," Althea mumbled. "I hope not. It sounds most uncomfortable."

Madame Zizette had the temerity to add, "But of course, your maid Colette will attend to her ladyship's coiffure, *non?*"

Althea was relieved when her mother responded to Madame Zizette's forwardness with a constrained smile rather than a rebuke. She was too grateful for the woman's handiwork to see her set down.

In the meantime, the particularly heavy showers of April gave way to a May of meadows and hedgerows alive with the miracle of new life. Althea thought the wildflowers seemed to grow more profusely than in previous years, and the music of songbirds resonated with a greater joy, giving her a feeling that the whole of nature was attending a celebration to which she had not been invited.

Her duties as mistress of Camberly Hall became onerous, and when entertaining members of the gentry, rather than joining in their conversation she gave herself over to woolgathering. Sometimes, when responding to a question that had been posed to her, she would notice that her answer would be met with a raising of brows followed by an exchange of puzzled glances.

On one such evening, after the last of her guests, Squire Collins, the local magistrate, had finally taken his leave, she turned to bid her mother good night in time to see that her obligatory smiles of farewell had been replaced by a perplexed frown.

"Perhaps you will tell me what is going on," the dowager ventured.

Althea raised a brow. "Please be more explicit, Mama. To what are you referring?"

"Pah!" she replied. "I am surpised you find occasion to ask. I am talking about your strange conduct of late."

"My conduct? I have done nothing untoward."

"No? Mary Swann expressed her pleasure in the fact that after fourteen years or so in the building, the Lyceum Theater was finally completed."

"I fail to see——"

"Let me finish. When asked if you shared her delight in the operas staged there, you replied, 'If something is not done about the unrest taking place at the docks, we are liable to have a full-scale insurrection on our hands.' Would you like me to continue?"

Althea covered her brow and slumped into a vacant footman's chair. "No. You paint a most mortifying picture."

She gave her mother a beseeching look. "Mama, what do you suppose is the matter with me? Am I going mad?"

Celeste bestowed a kiss on her cheek. "*La, non, ma petite.* Not in the way you imply."

Althea grasped at a locket pinned to her dress. "Please do not speak in riddles, Mama."

"Answer me this, child. Do you have trouble going to sleep at night"

Althea nodded.

"And find yourself daydreaming at the most inappropriate of times? For example, when you should be paying close attention to the conversations taking place at your own soirees?"

"You know I do," Althea replied, feeling perfectly wretched.

"Then, no doubt you also have this dreadful yearning for goodness-knows-what."

"I do? Yes. Of course I do. Mama, are you sure this does not bespeak of the first stages of madness?"

Celeste pulled her up from the chair and hugged her. "*Mais non*, my little cabbage. If you were a little more French and a lot less English, you would have realized right away that you are suffering from a madness of the heart, not of the mind."

Althea felt baffled, not comprehending the meaning of her words.

Celeste pinched her cheek. "You are not deranged, my little innocent, you are in love." She put a finger to her chin and furrowed her brow. "Now, who could it be? Surely not George?"

Althea replied in what she hoped was a nonchalant manner. "There is no one. I am afraid in this you are hopelessly mistaken. I am probably in need of a spring tonic. What was it that nanny used to give me? Ah, yes. Brimstone and treacle. I hated it"

Without further ado, Althea bid her mother good night and climbed the stairs with all possible speed before the lady could put forth any argument to the contrary.

Once she had dismissed Lizzie, Althea resigned herself to another night comprising very little sleep and a good deal of pacing back and forth on the large Aubusson carpet covering the bedroom floor.

Althea climbed into the high four-poster and drew the green velvet curtains in an effort to shut out the rest of the world, and, perhaps, the strange discontent that seemed to plague her so.

Her sleep was shallow and fitful and an hour later, she was fully awakened by the barking of a distant dog. With a groan, she got out of bed to close a window she had left open the merest crack, hoping this would shut out the noise.

After fastening the latch of the window, she stopped to admire how the moonlight silvered the blossoms on a nearby tree. She was about to return to the inviting warmth of her bed when in the direction of the river she saw a small light waving back and forth among the trees.

A smuggler's ruse, she thought. Before her father, the late earl, had made it unhealthy for them, smugglers plied their trade in the estuary as if it were a marketplace on a Saturday afternoon. She pressed her lips together in a grim line.

In their arrogance they presumed that now that a woman held the reins, they were free to come and go as they pleased. Althea was determined to make this assumption their undoing. She resolved to flush them out even if she had to hire a small army to do so.

Even as these ideas formulated in her mind, the light ceased to swing back and forth and then was abruptly extinguished. Althea shrugged and returned to her bed, determined to confer with her steward over the matter first thing in the morning.

Suddenly the creak of a floorboard sounded from the hallway and she got out of her bed once more, all thoughts of sleep quickly forgotten.

She opened her door in time to see her mother about to descend the staircase. Althea put on a pair of shoes and, donning a dark blue wool pelisse, followed her headstrong parent as quietly as she could. She reasoned that speed was not of the essence since she had a good idea where the lady was bound.

As Althea neared the riverbank she heard the sound of low-pitched voices. One definitely masculine, in spite of being barely above a whisper, the other the unmistakable lilt of her mother's beautiful voice.

Althea observed the couple from behind a screen of bushes. Their faces were obscured by the shadows of the tree under which they were standing. However, it was plain to see that her mother's companion was only an inch or two over average height; therefore, he could not possibly be Viscount Ridley, for he towered over most gentlemen of Althea's acquaintance.

This particular intelligence added considerably to Althea's peace of mind, as did the fact that the pair maintained a respectable distance between them. *Whatever else he is to Mama,* she reasoned, *he most certainly is not her lover.*

Reassured that Celeste was in no danger, she moved farther away, despising herself for having spied upon her. "Even so," she whispered, "I would do far worse to protect Mama from harm."

Althea made sure her mother had reentered the safety of the house before returning to her own room. Even if she had fallen asleep the moment her head hit the pillow, too much of the night had passed for Althea to get a full night's sleep. Unfortunately, sleep eluded her once more, giving her plenty of time to ponder the reason for her mother's odd behavior.

Chapter 5

As John partook of a breakfast of eggs and gammon at The Boar's Head late the following morning, he found that with each savory mouthful, his spirits rose one more notch. It was not his habit to eat breakfast there for he did not wish to bump into departing morning travelers, so before walking over from the cottage he had taken care not to arrive too early.

As a rule, he broke his fast at the cottage, usually a meal of bread and cold meat he brought with him from the boat. This morning he had awakened to discover that the ham he had hoped to have for breakfast was flyblown. Thoroughly disgusted, John stormed out of the cottage and paced back and forth along the seashore for a couple of hours.

Up to that point, John had convinced himself that he did not mind spending the occasional night in the miserable hovel. He had taken the trouble to furnish the wooden cot with a comfortable pallet, and had made an uneasy truce with the rodents he heard scuffling and squeaking in the walls at night.

It was opening the sturdy oak chest he used to keep his food safe from the rats, to find his breakfast being devoured by equally disgusting interlopers, that triggered within him a gut-wrenching despair and discontent for every level of his life.

In comparison, the inn seemed to be a haven of warmth and comfort. He gave the leather pouch he had strapped under his clothes a reassuring pat. It contained both gold and jewels the older Lady Camberly had entrusted into his care the previous night, items donated at considerable sacrifice by her ladyship and other French emigres.

It was his job to see that the contents reached Talleyrand, the one-time Bishop of Atun and ex-minister of foreign affairs for the French. Talleyrand was secretly plotting the overthrow of Napoleon Bonaparte with a view to restoring the Bourbons to the French throne.

Personally, John despised Talleyrand and his self-serving ways and hated to see Celeste Markham and her friends squander their money on what he deemed to be a lost cause.

He clenched his hands at the thought. He thought the Earl of Camberly's widow was the bravest woman he had ever encountered. Last year, in the middle of all the political turmoil taking place in France, Marcus had prevailed upon him to smuggle her into France to consult with Talleyrand in the matter of conspiring toward the deposing of Bonaparte.

Behind her facade of feminine charm lurked a core of fierce mother-love. Convinced that Napoleon intended to conquer the British Isles, Celeste vowed to sacrifice her life, if needs be, to prevent her daughter Althea from having to flee for her life as she had during the French Revolution.

In return for the help she received, it was at her insistence that when necessary, she would be a liaison between Marcus and the man she knew as John Soames. In exchange, John brought her messages from Talleyrand. It was in response to the luxury-loving Frenchman's demands that John was about to deliver for the hard-put-to exiles yet another offering of gold and jewels.

John's reverie was broken by the obsequious tenor of the innkeeper's voice.

"Good morning, sir. I trust our humble accommodations afforded you a comfortable night's sleep?"

This query from the landlord was met with silence. John presumed that either the person thus addressed had answered with a nod, or had spent a night that defied description. John's amusement at the thought quickly disappeared when the door to the saloon creaked open.

Cursing himself for having tarried so long, John slumped into his chair, thankful that the lower half of his face was obscured by several days' growth of beard. The sound of heavy boots on the wooden floor came to a sudden halt directly behind John's chair; resigning himself to the inevitable, he rose to face the newcomer.

It was his brother Marcus, who seemed to be viewing him with amused disbelief. "Mr. Soames, is it not? My good man, I hardly recognized you behind all that stubble." His words were those of a high-in-the-instep lord addressing an inferior. His expression even more so.

He reminded John of a sleek, well-groomed cat, one who had not had the occasion to lose his breakfast to the breeding endeavors of a fecund fly. And if the clear blue of his eyes was anything to go by, most certainly he had not been subjected to a fitful sleep due to the nocturnal activities of rats.

"My lord," he replied, "I am overcome by your gracious condescension." He embellished the sarcasm with an elaborate bow.

"I should hope so," Marcus replied, making a great display of examining his fingernails. "I surprise myself from time to time."

Before John could add to this, Marcus became all business and with voice lowered, queried, "Tell me, brother, what brings you here so early? I did not expect you to land until later this afternoon."

"One might ask the same of you." John sat down and gestured for Marcus to do likewise.

Marcus complied, pushed John's plate to one side, and replied, "I arrived here late last night. Thought that first I would visit Aunt Gertrude, then pay my respects to the ladies of Camberly Hall this morning prior to meeting you. Afterwards, I intend to push on to Brighton. Promised Prinny I would put in an appearance."

"Did you, now? The sacrifices you make do much to commend you. If I had known you were going to pay a visit to the Hall this morning, the older Lady Camberly and I could have remained snug in our respective beds last night."

"Really? I wish she would not persist in that little fantasy with that opportunist. I doubt Talleyrand makes too many sacrifices for the cause. I understand he lives very well under that so-called egalitarian regime."

"I quite agree," John rejoined. "In my opinion, the journey she subjected herself to last year was completely unnecessary. Sleeping in barns and under hedgerows and not one complaint passing her lips—not so much as a peep. Her sanity might be put to question, but I challenge anyone to deny her fortitude."

"Quite so. But I am afraid you will have to disappoint your heroine this time."

John raised a brow. "Oh?"

"Fraid so. You are bound for Portugal."

John raised both brows. "Portugal? Wellington's busy digging ditches north of Lisbon, is he not?"

"Not for much longer." Marcus handed a sealed document to John. "Burn this if you find yourself treed—otherwise, see that you put this in Wellington's hands, no one else's."

"I say, roaming around France is one thing. I know the language and can emulate most dialects, but I would be in over my head in Portugal."

"It will not be necessary for you to pose as a native. Just go to Wellington's camp at Torres Vedras or thereabouts and give him the damned letter."

"I understand. There is no need to be so bloody testy. I thought you had people who did this job blindfolded and wondered why you chose to involve me, that's all."

Marcus sighed. "It is precisely because you are unknown that you were chosen for the task. Now stop trying my patience, brother, and get on with it. The *Corinth* will be leaving the Port of London in five days on the early tide. Please don't miss it."

John nodded and rose to leave.

Marcus caught his sleeve. "Wait. You forgot to give me the lady's package. I shall be delighted to return it to her for you."

"Was there any doubt?" A picture of Marcus being regaled with refreshments by a beautiful lady and her probably equally lovely daughter tinged his response with sarcasm. He retrieved the package from his canvas pouch and handed it over to Marcus, replacing it with the letter intended for the Duke of Wellington.

"Anything else before I leave?"

Marcus smiled. "As a matter of fact, there is one small detail

I forgot to mention."

"And what might that be?" John asked, dreading to hear the answer.

"You will be traveling as befits an English gentleman, so naturally, your man Jenkins will be able to accompany you."

John spent a moment or two savoring the thought of the niceties that went with rank and privilege. "Are you sure?"

"Of course. Too many of our friends are serving with Wellington to do otherwise and they will not read too much into your showing up. You have the reputation of being somewhat of a rover, you know."

"No, I did not know."

"Oh, yes. Since leaving Jamaica you have been toddling all over India. It explains that Gypsy complexion you have acquired."

"Does it? Tell me, Marcus, did I enjoy my little jaunt?"

"Absolutely, old chap. As a matter of fact, you cannot wait to get back."

John panicked. "I know nothing about India and people are bound to ask questions."

Marcus responded with an expansive gesture. "I shouldn't worry. I had some pamphlets prepared for you on the subject of ancient Hindu temples. And, oh yes, there is the matter of a tiger hunt you attended under the auspices of some raja or other. You'll find his name written down somewhere. You may study it all at your leisure while you are on the *Corinth*. Help you pass the time."

Marcus rose from the table and, presuming the interview to be over, John did likewise, not at all happy with the turn his life had taken.

That's it, he thought. *As soon as I get back, I am going to tell Marcus and his cronies in government to go to the devil. I fail to see how I have helped the cause in any way. Perhaps the money put in the right hands helped hasten the downfall of that damned policeman, Fouche, but I have my doubts—that rascal is his own worst enemy.*

Marcus shook his hand, then grimaced. "I suggest that the first thing you do on reaching the house in London is to soak in a nice, hot bath—two would be better." He scrutinized

John's face. "And for goodness' sake, have Jenkins shave off that ghastly fuzz. I cannot for the life of me understand how you could lower your standards in such a fashion. You look like the very dregs of society."

"That is the point, brother dear. One can hardly blend in with the aforementioned dregs dressed like one of Brummell's cronies, now can one? At least, and not live to be taking messages to Wellington."

Marcus raised a brow. "My—and you called *me* testy. Get out of the wrong side of the bed this morning, did we?"

John remembered his spoiled breakfast. "One could say so."

"Never mind. A good night's sleep at the London house will sort you out Jenkins has everything in hand. Your clothes ready to go and the necessary money to pay for the trip. Reliable chap you have there."

Without more ado, Marcus took his leave, stopping at the door to bestow upon John a breezy wave of farewell. As the door slammed, John gritted his teeth, taking umbrage at the way Marcus chose not to see the wretched life he had thrust upon his only brother while on the other hand, his own had not changed one iota.

One thing he was sure of. He would not get a shave until he was good and ready.

Determined to put the problem of her mother's nocturnal escapades to the back of her mind for the time being, Althea spent the morning conferring with the housekeeper, Mrs. Denchforth. She had made a spot-check of some of the rarely used guest chambers in the east wing, and having detected a decided scent of mustiness in several, ordered a general airing and cleaning of a dozen or so of the rooms.

On being dismissed, the housekeeper, apparently smarting from the imagined disparagement of her domestic skills, pulled eight of the chambermaids from their usual duties. She delivered a blistering tirade, pointing out their shortcomings in the field of domestic service, then sent them scurrying to the east wing of the Hall to rectify the matter of the neglected guest chambers. She followed at a statelier pace, her ample bosom thrust forward in what Althea presumed to be outraged dignity.

Althea sighed, and returned to her own apartments. She had not meant to lay criticism at Mrs. Denchforth's door. Given the dampness of the English climate, it took no time at all for an empty chamber to take on a whiff of mildew. Try as she might, Althea thought she would never be able to achieve that all-important rapport with servants that contributed toward harmony both above- and below-stairs.

On entering her chambers, Lizzie, who was closely scrutinizing the lace on one of Althea's morning dresses, looked up and smiled. "Had a set-to with the old she-dragon have you, my lady? That woman has one girl or another reduced to tears nearly every waking hour."

Althea forbore to remind her abigail that she should not be so forward, and at no time should be referring to the housekeeper in such a disparaging manner.

Lizzie enjoyed such liberties on the strength of a friendship between them that harked back to when they were both in leading strings. As the gatekeeper's daughter, she had grown up in the house, which was an integral part of the massive granite portals to the estate, and sometimes had been the only child on hand of Althea's age for her to play with.

Althea had never formed as close a friendship with children of her own class as she had with Lizzie. When she outgrew her need for a nanny, rather than seeing her friend toiling in a menial position below-stairs, Althea had insisted on having Lizzie for her personal maid. On becoming mistress of Camberly Hall, she had offered her friend the more exalted position of lady's companion.

"What would my duties be?" Lizzie had asked.

"Duties? None, as such. It would be as it sounds. You would be my friend and companion and accompany me on my charitable rounds in the village, and also travel with me. When this terrible war with the French is over, we could visit the Continent. We should have a jolly time."

Lizzie looked pensive. "I see. I would have nothing to do but trail after you, pretending I was gentry? Sup at your table, too, I suppose?"

Althea nodded.

Lizzie shook her head. "You mean well, madam, but I cannot take kindly to the idea."

"I fail to see why."

"Begging your pardon, it is just as well that I cannot."

"Oh?"

"Let me explain. First of all, I am not suited for such a position. If I had to eat with my betters I would choke to death on the first bite." Lizzie stressed this point with a grimace. "I don't relish the idea at all. Take, for instance, this sitting on my bottom all day while some other female tends to your needs—fair gives me the shudders, it does."

Althea had seen the wisdom in Lizzie's words and pursued the subject no further, resigned to the fact that at least in private, their friendship was worth the price of accepting Lizzie's occasional lapses of propriety.

Now, on this particular morning, Althea watched Lizzie thread a needle and apply herself to sewing the lace back on the hem of her dress. It occurred to her that whereas Lizzie might lack the flair for styling hair that her mother's abigail, Colette, possessed, no one could fault her skill with a sewing needle.

In what seemed to be no time at all, Lizzie finished the task and, wielding a pair of small, ivory-handled scissors, snipped the thread with a triumphant flourish. "There," she said, displaying her work for Althea to admire. "Good as new."

Althea concurred, then concealed a tiny yawn behind the back of her hand.

Lizzie gave her a quizzical stare, then said, "Good gracious, you look terrible. I hope you are not coming down with the grippe. Mary Grimes, Lady Alcott's maid, told me it was making the rounds."

She dropped the dress on a chair and took Althea firmly by the jaw and stared into her eyes, a worried look on her face. "Those circles under your eyes make you look like a raccoon.

I can't think why I didn't notice them before. You know, Lord Alcott was taken real poorly. Before his fever broke they feared he would die."

Althea pulled away from Lizzie's grip. "Such is not the case with me, so stop worrying. I am merely suffering from a lack of sleep, a condition I hope to rectify by going to bed early this evening."

"Am I right in thinking that you have finished seeing to the household staff?"

"Well, yes," Althea replied, wondering where the conversation was leading.

"And you're not thinking of delivering soup to the old widows of the village, are you?"

"No, not today."

"Then there is no reason why you cannot remove your outer garments and take a nice nap on your daybed, is there?"

"I suppose not. But…"

"Then I would be shirking my duty if I did not see to it that you got out of those clothes and did so, wouldn't I?"

Without waiting for a reply, Lizzie proceeded to untie the back of Althea's dress and did not leave the room until her mistress was lying on the daybed with a quilt tucked about her.

Althea had been somewhat irritated by Lizzie's high-handed actions but as she snuggled under the coverlet, had to admit that she was grateful to be there. It did not take long for sleep to descend upon her like a dark, warm cloud and sweep her into a series of dreams, none of which reached a conclusion, but rather, skipped from one improbable scene to another.

Ultimately, she found herself walking on Camberly pier, painfully aware that she was wearing her nightclothes with a cloak of scarlet satin flung carelessly over her shoulders. Even while dreaming, it occurred to her that she had never owned such a garish garment in her life.

To add to her shame, an angel with light brown hair hovered over her, a sorrowful look on his face. Suddenly a gust of wind tore the cape from her shoulders, leaving her exposed to the shocked expressions on the faces of several passersby who suddenly appeared out of nowhere.

The angel descended in front of her and seemed to grow to an enormous size, blocking all avenues of escape.

"If you dared to be beautiful, this never would have happened," he scolded. To her consternation, his face transformed into that of the impudent mariner she had encountered on the pier earlier in April; then his huge form slowly faded away until there was nothing left of him save a faint wisp of smoke.

Althea was in the process of making her escape from the pier, running past a host of strangers all eyeing her with great disdain, when she was awakened by the sound of an angry voice.

The booming stentor, puffed up with its own sense of importance, could only be that of her great-uncle, the Marquis de Maligny. It seemed to come from directly outside the door to her own chambers, heralding his return to Camberly Hall like a tantara of trumpets.

"Be careful with my trunk, you clumsy peasant," he roared. "It cannot be replaced in this sorry country."

The prince's soiree at the Pavilion in Brighton would not be taking place until the first week in June, so for him to forsake London could only mean that invitations to participate in the social round had ceased to flow.

Althea's musings on the subject were interrupted by the sound of Lizzie's voice countering that of the marquis. Lizzie was the only person in her employ who was not intimidated by the Frenchman's arrogant manner of dealing with servants.

"If you please, my lord, Lady Camberly is getting a much-needed sleep, and I am sure you would not wish to disturb her."

Althea was relieved that Lizzie did not add fuel to his irascible mood by adding anything further. She surmised that his foul humor was brought upon by a flare-up of his rheumatism, no doubt the result of a damp April.

He uttered a grumbling response to Lizzie's objections, but by then he was too far down the hall for Althea to catch the rest of his words.

That evening at dinner he lost no time in voicing his outrage at the appalling lack of respect he had received at the hands of her maid.

"Why, if any servant on my estate had dared to show half the effrontery, they would have been sent packing to die of starvation in some ditch, and not before having the skin flayed off their impudent hides, I might add." As he spoke, his face grew red with indignation.

Celeste spared Althea the trouble of a response by taking up the gauntlet in her stead. "Perhaps, Uncle, if you and the rest of the French aristocrats had dealt with their peasants in a more humane manner, it is quite possible that this evening, you would be dining under your own roof and not subjecting poor Althea to your constant criticism of all things English."

The marquis put down his napkin and stood up. "You overstep yourself, niece. If I had not taken the trouble to save you, you would not be alive this day to hurl such abuse upon my head, and 'poor Althea' would not be here to witness your ghastly behavior."

Seemingly unruffled by the vituperation directed toward her, Celeste countered, "I think Althea would be here. She might have looked a little different, of course, but not much. She is inclined to favor her father in looks—and in disposition too, thank God. You see, Uncle, I do not deny that my behavior is ghastly. We de Malignys are a dreadful lot, would you not agree?"

Althea held her breath, wondering how much further her mother could provoke their kinsman before she found his hands around her throat. She just wished both of them would exercise within the walls of Camberly Hall the same restraint they managed to muster when moving among polite society.

To her relief, the marquis gave her mother a wry smile and sat down in his chair once more. *"Touché,* my dear. I will not admit to being dreadful, as you put it, but I suppose we French are inclined to get a trifle overheated. After all, we are not coldblooded Englishmen."

"Uncle Jean-Claude! You have done it again. Now apologize to Althea."

Althea waved him off. "Please do not concern yourself, sir.

I know full well that you are a sham, and do not mean half the things you say at this table. Pray let us finish dinner, and Mama and I will leave you to your cognac and cigars."

"Yes, Uncle darling, please do, although it is a shame our dear Philippe is not here to keep you company. When do you expect him back from Bedfordshire?"

The marquis smiled at the mention of his grandson. "You may be sure that he will return in good time to attend the prince's soiree. I am sure he would have returned home a lot sooner, but his late mother's father takes advantage of his sweet nature and makes it very difficult for him to leave."

"Philippe should develop more backbone," Celeste inserted.

"It is not that easy. That dreadful man holds Philippe's inheritance over his head like a weapon. The baron claims that should he die, Philippe would be ill prepared to run Bainbridge Manor after him. He is constantly drumming into the poor boy's head matters that are far better left in the hands of a good steward."

"I am sure Lord Bainbridge means no harm," Althea rejoined. "He must be dreadfully lonely since his wife died. Philippe is the only one left for him to cling to in his old age."

"That is no excuse. The man should pull himself together and get on with it. I would not dream of interfering in Philippe's life in such a manner."

"Of course you would not, Uncle dear," Celeste said, casting an impish smile in Althea's direction. "You are far too sophisticated to indulge in such petty tyrannies."

Althea held her breath, wondering how he would react to her mother's tongue-in-cheek remark. Apparently it went right over his head, because he responded with a preening smile.

Althea exhaled. She should have known that her uncle held too smug a belief in his own perfection not to take a compliment at face value. In any case, the family spat had blown over as swiftly as a summer squall. She deemed it a mercy that the French contingency of the family could end such dreadful scenes seemingly without bearing grudges, one to the other.

Once alone with her mother, Althea was tempted to bring

up the subject of her midnight tryst with the stranger, but could not bring herself to do so. This troubled Althea because she knew that it was something that had to be faced sooner or later. Because of her indecision, she ended up subjecting her mother to a very indifferent game of whist.

Chapter 6

As far as Althea was concerned, June arrived alarmingly soon. Cousin Philippe arrived home a scant three days before the Prince of Wales's soiree was to take place.

She had mixed feelings about attending the affair. She held up her dress in front of the pier glass in her dressing room several times before the event, marveling how well it seemed to suit her. However, in the back of her mind lurked the horrible fear that those attending the affair would deem the green-and-white dress cause for ridicule, not admiration.

She cast the dress upon the bed and shrugged. *It is too late to do anything about it now,* she thought. *I shall hold my head high and stare the dragons down.*

On the eve of the soiree, Althea and the other three members of her family and their personal servants set out for Brighton. Althea owned a well-appointed house there on the Marine Parade.

Like most of the neighboring houses, it boasted bow windows and was embellished with Corinthian columns. Her father had bought it in a rare fit of extravagance, deeming it only fair to provide his young wife with the summertime pleasures of Brighton.

Althea had mixed feelings over the honor for which her family had been singled out. She considered most of the prince's friends to be raffish and not quite respectable. However, the one time His Royal Highness had taken the time to converse with her at any length she had been pleasantly surprised at his erudition on diverse subjects. The prince was a gentleman with many facets to his character.

Their invitations to the pavilion were for five-thirty, much to the disgust of the marquis. It seemed that the Prince of Wales liked to dine at six-thirty.

That afternoon, it was Lizzie who coifed Althea's hair. Under Colette's tutelage, Lizzie had become adept at the task. Colette had convinced Althea to cut the front of her hair short so that it fell in tendrils to frame her face. The rest of her hair was dressed high on the crown of her head and bound with bands of pearls intertwined with a ribbon of white satin.

Knowing that she would likely question every attempt on Lizzie's part to change her appearance, Lizzie and Colette agreed that Althea should not be allowed to look at the results until she was securely tied and pinned into her dress.

When the moment finally came, her mother led her to the looking glass and cried, *"Voila!"*

Althea stared into the glass, momentarily speechless as she studied her reflection.

I actually look quite pretty, but it is just an illusion. Just clever little tricks that abigails use.

Finally she turned to her mother and said, "Mama, will not people think it odd of me to fuss so much?"

"Au contraire, ma petite. Mark my words, those present will wonder why it took you so long. Besides, you should not give a fig what others think. It is far too exhausting."

"Then you approve?"

"But of course, *chérie!* You look absolutely lovely. Do you not agree, Lizzie?"

Lizzie bobbed. "Oh, yes, ma'am. But I have always thought so."

Althea's eyes shone. "Mama, I am so looking forward to this evening and yet I am also filled with this deep dread. Why do you suppose this is?"

Celeste tapped her on the cheek with her fan. "Did I not tell you that it takes courage to be beautiful?"

Althea knitted her brows. "I must confess that I do not know what you mean. It is such an odd thing to say."

"Before this night is over, I am certain my meaning will have become crystal clear."

Althea turned from the tall glass and her self-absorption and noticed for the first time that her mother was an absolute vision in a gown of ivory-colored Pekin satin, a material distinguished by a subtle stripe in the weave. Save for a piping in the seams, the dress was free of adornment, the perfect setting for a magnificent emerald necklace and pendant earrings that intensified the green fire dancing in her eyes.

Althea never ceased to be in awe of her mother's beauty. "Mama, you must be the bravest woman in the world, for I declare, in all of Society there is none lovelier."

Celeste rewarded her with a dimpling smile. "Thank you, darling. What a charming compliment."

The marquis and Cousin Philippe were effusive with their compliments of both ladies' attire when they joined them downstairs. The marquis was elegantly attired in black. His coat fashioned of a heavy grained silk.

Philippe was similarly attired, save his waistcoat was more colorful, being made out of blue-and-silver brocade. Philippe was a handsome young man, tall and slender, with clear hazel eyes and hair as dark and glossy as a raven's wing.

They rode to the Marine Pavilion in a dark blue carriage, a fine-looking equipage with the family crest of three unicorn heads emblazoned on the side.

At that time, the Marine Pavilion was a dignified but plain structure, the focal point being a center dome flanked by a semiperistyle of Ionic columns and bow windows.

When they were ushered into the corridor, a long hall a hundred and sixty-two feet in length, Althea was struck by the fact that however often she saw it, the spectacle never ceased to amaze her.

She was overcome by the rich colors. Pinks and jades fought with blues and vermilions and golds for attention. Adorning the walls were murals of lush blue waves of bamboo painted against a background of a deep pink hue. Cabinets of satinwood fashioned to look like bamboo, their doors emblazoned with insects of magenta, were laden with brilliantly colored porcelain pieces.

Tables and chairs also made of satinwood fashioned to emulate bamboo, or lavishly adorned with intricately carved ormolu, lined the room. Every nook housed gilt statuary perched atop porcelain and ormolu plinths. Life-size figures dressed in luxuriously embroidered kimonos stood against the wall.

With equal disregard for the cost involved, magnificent staircases of wrought iron, also fashioned to emulate bamboo save for the handrails, which were made of mahogany, flanked each end of the corridor.

This rich array was repeated to infinity by the strategic placement of wall mirrors, causing Althea to be dizzied by the excess. She found the clash of colors unsettling, and wondered how their host could possibly wish to surround himself with such dazzling *éclat*.

A cursory scanning of the people who had arrived before her party proved to Althea's relief that their host was not numbered among them. Not counting the four members of her family, there were fourteen in number. Either there were more guests due to arrive, or it would prove to be a very intimate little group.

She noticed that as usual, the gentlemen huddled together in a corner, seemingly engaged in heated debate. Althea surmised that various aspects of the war taking place on the Iberian Peninsula were under discussion. She found it amusing how gentlemen who had never set foot in Spain or Portugal knew exactly how the war against the French should be waged.

Four of the ladies had paired off and were strolling the length of the corridor, chattering away like magpies, no doubt exchanging *on dits* regarding the peccadilloes of persons who had the misfortune not to be present to defend their good names.

The other three, aging beauties with faces heavily made up in the manner popular in the era of powdered wigs and panniered dresses, sat at an ornate gilt table with their heads bent towards each other, deep in earnest discussion. Their rouge bled from their lips and cheeks into a network of fine wrinkles, reminding Althea of dolls that had been left out in the rain before their paint had dried.

The tallest and the thinnest of the group she recognized as Margaret Greenleaf, the Earl of Whitbrook's wife, known for her vicious tongue. She had torn to shreds the reputation of more than one innocent. Usually, it was slyly suggested, ladies known to be diamonds of the first water.

To Althea's dismay, probably at the prompting of the harpy facing the entrance to the corridor, the marchioness had the effrontery to turn around and subject her to deep scrutiny through a diamond-studded quizzing glass. *Perhaps it is this sort of behavior that leads Mama to say that beauty requires courage,* she thought grimly.

As if reading her mind, Celeste squeezed her hand and said, "Remember, *ma petite*. Care not a fig and consign the beldam to the devil—if he will have her."

"Mon Dieu!" the marquis exclaimed. "Is *she* still alive? I had thought the Horned One to have claimed her years ago."

"The old chap is probably terrified at the prospect of the mischief she could cause," Philippe added.

"In which case," the marquis continued, "I fear the lady just might be the first human ever to achieve immortality."

Her fears allayed by their wicked humor, Althea relaxed, and as soon as their presence was announced, she raised her chin and glided into the room with all the regal dignity she could muster, her mother by her side, resolutely keeping pace.

The marquis and his grandson escorted them as far as the ladies promenading in their direction, then, with a few pleasantries and brief bows, scurried to join the other gentlemen.

A few minutes later, the arrival of a Mrs. Howard and her daughter Mavis was announced. Mrs. Howard was a fine-looking woman of an uncertain age, well endowed in the bosom with hair a suspiciously bright shade of red. By her appearance, it would seem that her daughter was well entrenched into a life of spinsterhood.

"Who are they?" Althea asked.

"Mrs. Howard is a colonel's widow," Celeste replied.

"How sad. Lost his life in this dreadful war, did he?"

Celeste nodded. "At Trafalgar."

Althea knitted her brow. "But I have never encountered the lady before."

"I should not wonder. But now that His Highness has singled the Howards out with special attention, I suspect you will see them everywhere."

Althea put Mavis Howard under close scrutiny. "I say. She is hardly the sort of female for whom I thought His Highness would harbor a *tendre.*"

Her mother raised a brow. "And never would," she whispered. "It is the *mother* who has captured his interest"

Althea's eyes grew wide. "But she must be several years older than the prince."

"Really, child, how can you have reached your fourth Season in Society and not know that our prince has a weakness for matrons?"

Althea gasped. "Surely not."

"Do not look so shocked. I suspect that of late, his attachments are more platonic in nature. A little motherly sympathy along with his brandy must be very soothing."

Before Althea could answer, she was surprised to hear George Delville's name being announced. She wondered how someone of George's lack of consequence had managed to be numbered among the very cream of the *ton*.

It did not take her long to find out. After a searching glance down the corridor, George made a beeline towards Althea and her mother, whereupon he made a deep bow to the older Lady Camberly with an accompanying effusive greeting before turning his attention to Althea.

His jaw immediately dropped.

"I say! Do forgive me. I did not recognize you for the moment."

Althea gave him a cold stare. "Really, Mr. Delville? How odd."

"I meant nothing untoward, your ladyship," he responded, echoing her formal manner of address. "It's just that you look so dashed beautiful and I was not paying close attention. It is quite understandable, I am sure."

Althea dismissed him with a brief nod and turned her attention to her mother. George hovered about, looking absolutely miserable. Realizing that he was too intimidated to join the lofty ranks of the other gentlemen, Althea took pity on him and accorded him a brief smile.

George snapped up the offered crumb like a starving puppy. "I say. I did so enjoy your ball last spring. It was the crush of the Season, don't you know?"

Without taking a breath, he plunged headlong into a topic so beloved by any right-minded person in possession of even the slightest drop of English blood. "By the way, this has been a glorious day for so early in June. Would you not agree?"

Althea leaned forward and whispered, "For goodness' sake, calm down, George. These people do not bite—at least, not in the literal sense, and I doubt they will subject you to any unpleasantness."

George looked crestfallen. "No, I suppose not. I lack the consequence to even be noticed. I wish the Prince of Wales had not invited me. These intimate little affairs are far more difficult to handle than a crush."

"Cheer up," Althea soothed. "Having the good will of Prinny should give you enormous cachet. To what do you owe your good fortune, do you suppose?"

"Baron Lampson invited me to a ball they hosted directly after you left Town in such a hurry. Prinny happened to overhear a comment I made with regard to Beau Brummel's neck linen."

Althea raised a brow. "Oh? Please elucidate."

"I would rather not. But you must have noticed that of late, the points of Brummell's collars and the elaborate fall of his cravats have reached such impractical extremes he can scarcely move his head."

George took on a haunted look. "Just let us say that it was not the sort of remark a chap wishes to be known for, and it was but the merest whisper in Francis Lampton's ear. Imagine my horror when I heard this great guffaw directly behind me and turned to face no less a personage than the Prince of Wales, taking high glee in my remark."

"I have heard that Mr. Brummell's odd behavior toward the prince of late is driving a wedge between them."

"But do you not see? The prince has accorded me his regard on the strength of this one remark. Good heavens, Althea, I am not a great wit. I am not likely to trot out another syllable worthy of note if I were to outlive Methuselah."

Althea laughed in spite of herself. "You underestimate yourself, George. Just be you. His Royal Highness is a kind man and will do nothing to hurt you, but in future please be more circumspect. It does not do to make powerful enemies."

George bowed, and with his brow knitted as if weighing her words, took his leave of the ladies to join the other gentlemen. Althea shot her mother a rueful glance. "Poor George. The kind regard of our illustrious prince is on the verge of killing him."

"Do not concern yourself, darling. George will survive. The worst that can happen is that invitations from the prince will taper off. Who knows? Perhaps your childhood friend is destined to become the darling of the *ton.*"

"Mama, do you really think so?"

"Hardly."

"Oh, dear."

The next guest to arrive was Lord Ridley. At the time, Althea was engaged in a polite exchange of chitchat with a young matron she had known since childhood. It had not taken Althea long to discover that they no longer met on common ground and had very little to say to one another.

Elizabeth married her husband, a Mr. Henry Beaton, one of the Prince of Wales's cronies, during her and Althea's very first Season. As Beau Brummell put it, "Before her dancing slippers had begun to show signs of wear."

Her first child, a little girl, was born a scant nine months later, causing many a raised brow among the more raffish members of the *ton.* Their second child, a son, was just three months old. When news of the second baby's birth was mentioned at White's, Mr. Brummell expressed surprise. "Did not think Beaton was home often enough to accomplish the deed."

As Elizabeth Beaton enthused *ad nauseum* about her children,

Althea watched the viscount's progress down the corridor out of the corner of her eye. She was surprised when he accorded her mother only the very briefest of bows. She wondered if their friendship was cooling. Marcus Ridley was not known for steadfast devotion.

Just about the time that the young matron's droning had driven Althea into a state of glassy-eyed desperation, the arrival of His Royal Highness was announced. Elizabeth ceased her chatter in midsentence and hastened to her husband's side. Thankful for the reprieve, Althea joined her mother.

At the same time, those who were seated rose to their feet, and all heads turned to watch the prince's laborious descent down the staircase. As she made her curtsey along with the rest of the ladies, Althea noted that the heir to the throne's girth had increased even more since the last London Season.

Charming to a fault, the prince made his way along the corridor, according each guest his full attention as he exchanged pleasantries with him or her.

When it was the turn of the Camberly ladies to be so honored, he addressed Althea first. "My dear, you have blossomed into one of Society's beauties, I see." This remark was followed by a twinkling smile. "Splendid. Splendid. A lovely lady is one of the Deity's more lavish gifts to the world."

Feeling her face flush with a mixture of pleasure and embarrassment at being singled out for such effusive praise, Althea mumbled her thanks. Immediately, she castigated herself for sounding like an idiotic pea-goose and frantically searched her mind for something intelligent to say. It was too late. The prince directed his next remark to her mother.

"Lady Camberly. It is always a pleasure to meet you—nay, an honor."

This remark was made in a voice barely above a whisper. Raising his voice to a normal pitch, he went on to expound on the plans he had for extending the Pavilion; then, with a bow, he moved on to the next guests, who happened to be Mrs. Howard and her spinster daughter.

Promptly at half past six, dinner was announced. Their

host approached the highest-ranking lady in the room—on this occasion it was the Marchioness of Whitbrook—and with a bow, offered her his arm. He then escorted her in to dinner, his guests pairing up and following behind them.

The dinner, as Althea expected, was comprised of a steady stream of courses and removes, accompanied by the appropriate wines. She took care to take only a small sampling of everything placed before her and partook of the merest sip of each wine, yet still managed to leave the table feeling horribly uncomfortable.

Afterwards the prince, well fortified by brandy and wine, entertained his guests with anecdotes in the large, round-shaped drawing room known as the Saloon. The laughter he garnered from wickedly mimicking the voices and foibles of their mutual political enemies drowned out the strains of a string quartet emanating from an adjoining room.

Amid the frivolity, Althea experienced subtle overtures from two of the younger gentlemen, both of them married, one of them, to her distress, Henry Beaton, the husband of the voluble Elizabeth. This made her feel extremely uncomfortable and more than a little insulted. At first, she wondered if a too-cordial manner on her part had led the pair to believe that she was receptive to such suggestions, but a roguish wink from Mr. Beaton soon changed her mind.

According him a freezing stare, she rose and departed the room with the intention of seeking sanctuary in the gardens. While walking along the corridor, passing several footmen in the process, she happened to catch a glimpse of her image in one of the mirrors lining the wall. For a brief moment, she did not recognize herself, having forgotten the transformation her new dress and coiffure had brought about.

Suddenly her mother's words made sense. It did indeed take courage to be beautiful. Along with the pleasant compliments and special deference one received, one also had to fight off the dishonorable overtures of out-and-out bounders. Althea wondered if the good outweighed the bad.

She was still debating this point when the sound of rapid steps coming in her direction gave her cause to fear that one of her would-be seducers was hot in pursuit. A backward glance proved it was George Delville. With a sigh of relief, she waited for him to catch up.

Having done so, he looked about him and, jerking his head in the direction of a nearby footman who stood with his eyes fixed to the ceiling, said, "I think it would be prudent to move further down."

Althea complied, wondering at George's need for privacy.

George ran a finger along the edge of his cravat and cleared his throat. It had always been Althea's experience that such an act was usually a prelude to a situation she would rather avoid.

"Well, George?" she prodded.

To her dismay, he grabbed her hand. "Dear, dear, Althea, I must confess a love and passion for you that will not be quenched. Please tell me that my suit is not without hope."

Althea snatched her hand away. "Oh, for heaven's sake, George, behave yourself. I fear it is the wine that fans your ardor, not love."

George retrieved her hand. "I swear it is otherwise. The moment I saw you this evening, I fell completely and utterly in love with you."

Althea pulled her hand from his grasp once more. "Nonsense. I am the person I have always been. Nothing in my attitude towards life has changed that could possibly make you love me."

"I have always considered you to be kind and considerate—now my eyes have been opened to your beauty."

"Oh, dear. This evening is proving to be full of revelations. I, too, am viewing things in a new light."

George's eyes filled with hope. "Can it be that my love is returned?"

Althea shook her head. "I wish I could say otherwise, but your sort of love is far too shallow to last."

"How can you say that? Your refusal leaves me absolutely desolate."

"You will get over it, George. If you truly regarded me with love, you would have considered me to be beautiful long before this."

"But—"

"Pray let me finish. A woman's beauty fades with age and, I fear, so will your love. I rather think that you would become yet another man who ogles young girls behind his unsuspecting wife's back. I would not want that—would you?"

"Oh, I *say*." George stared at her gape-mouthed, reminding Althea of a fish gasping for air.

In a wave of pity, she patted his arm. "Just because we would not rub well together as husband and wife does not mean we cannot remain good friends, does it?"

"I suppose not," George answered, his mouth turned down in a sulk.

"Splendid." Even to Althea, her response sounded far too effusive. "If you hurry back, no one will suspect that anything out of the ordinary has taken place."

George seemed relieved, and with a curt nod, wheeled around and returned to the gathering in the drawing room. As he opened the door, Althea heard the unmistakable sound of their host's strong baritone waft into the corridor as he sang one of the popular songs of the moment. It would seem that the festivities were well under way and it was highly unlikely that she would be missed for a while.

Althea walked the length of the corridor before finding access to the garden via a small anteroom. Once out in the night air, she covered a considerable distance, regretting the thinness of her slippers as the heavy dew on the grass seeped through the soles, soaking her stocking feet in a manner she found most disagreeable.

She had thought to sit on one of the garden benches before returning to the drawing room, but since they proved to be equally bedewed, she changed her mind and decided to rejoin the others.

As she retraced her steps, she heard voices coming from the midst of a small shrubbery. First, she heard the deep baritone of a man. The answering voice was soft and feminine, and all too familiar.

Althea was filled with foreboding. *Oh, no. What on earth could Mama possibly be up to now?*

Hating herself for doing so, a backward glance confirmed her worst fears. Her mother was not a small woman, yet the man's form towered over her. It had to be Marcus Ridley—no other man present that evening could begin to match his stature. Then Althea noticed that although the two of them stood quite close, they did not touch one another. Not one gesture passed between them that could be considered untoward.

She quickened her pace across the lawn, thankful that the background roar of the ocean and a rising breeze rustling through the trees covered up the sound of her footsteps. As she tried to make sense of her mother's odd behavior, she found she could come to only one conclusion.

Mama and I are going to have a talk before we retire this evening, and neither of us is going to bed until I am satisfied with her answers.

Chapter 7

Confronting her mother proved not to be easy. But then, Althea had not expected it to be. At first, Celeste adopted the stance of a mother dealing with an impudent child, her four-inch advantage over Althea serving her well. This ploy might have worked, but as head of the family, Althea knew it was up to her to protect their interests.

Althea also knew that her mother might skirt the truth by omission, but was certain that she was too honorable to tell her a deliberate falsehood. Althea gritted her teeth and prepared for a sleepless night.

Finally Celeste capitulated—to a degree. "Darling, this is all my fault. Had I been a little better at this sort of thing, you would never have found out, but having done so, it is only natural that you would want to know what is going on."

"Then you will tell me?"

"Alas, I do not have that authority."

"Then who does, pray? Lord Ridley?"

Celeste shrugged. "It is possible. I cannot say for sure."

Althea put her hand to her mouth. "Mama, in what sort of situation have you put yourself?"

"Oh, for goodness' sake, child, do not exaggerate the matter. I shall summon Marcus to attend us later in the afternoon, and I am sure he will enlighten you."

"It cannot be put off in such a manner. I wish to see him as soon as possible—directly after breakfast, if it can be arranged."

Celeste frowned. "Now you are being tiresome, child. It is almost dawn, and I do not intend to break my fast until well past noon. Now be a good little cabbage and kindly leave my chamber. I wish to go to bed."

"I am sorry, Mama. But first, I am afraid I must prevail upon you to write your letter. I shall leave it with the footman on duty with instructions that it is to be delivered to Lord Ridley at the earliest hour you deem proper. Ten o'clock should suit, do you not agree?"

"No, I do not. And you may be sure that his lordship would not, either."

Althea sighed. "Very well. Make it eleven o'clock. Not a moment later. Where should it be directed?"

"To the pavilion, of course. He is always a guest of the prince's when visiting Brighton."

"Of course," Althea echoed, then covered a yawn with her hand.

"For goodness' sake, Althea, go to bed at once. Be assured that I will take care of the letter."

"It hardly seems fair. You must be every bit as tired as I."

Celeste made a shooing gesture. "To bed with you. I am not in the least bit tired. One can get past it, you know."

Althea kissed her on the cheek and returned to her own room. As she pulled the coverlet up to her chin, she heard the distant sound of a rooster crowing. With a groan, she turned over and buried her face in the pillow.

Lord Ridley was ushered into the drawing room that afternoon promptly at four o'clock. While the housekeeper was present, they exchange pleasantries during which their visitor politely refused Althea's offer of refreshments.

As soon as the servant withdrew from the room, Marcus Ridley stood up. "It is quite pleasant outdoors. I suggest we conduct this matter in your garden where there is less chance of being overheard. It has been my experience that for the lack of anything better to do, the staff of seldom-used establishments develops an inordinate interest in the affairs of their betters."

The thought crossed Althea's mind that the servants of any establishment of the viscount's, seldom-used or otherwise, would have little opportunity to be bored, given the constant stream of love-struck females purported to pass through those portals. Althea immediately regretted the lack of charity that prompted such a thought. Lord Ridley had always shown her every kindness and consideration.

"A wise decision, to be sure, Lord Ridley."

"I am glad you agree. Now if I can prevail upon you to consider me a friend, I should like us to be on a first-name basis."

"Very well, Lord Ridley."

"Marcus."

"Marcus," Althea echoed. "Forgive me. It might take me a while to get used to calling you that."

He responded with a slight nod.

As the trio walked through the garden, stopping every few steps to make a show of inspecting a shrub or sniffing a flower, Marcus gave Althea a concise reprise of what was taking place.

Afterwards, Althea sat down on a garden bench, numb with shock. Finally she turned to Celeste. "It was not possible for you to have visited Paris last year. All your time is accounted for."

Celeste rolled her eyes. "Althea, how can you be so naive? All it took was careful planning, a modicum of deceit, and a good friend who is far too romantic for her own good, and there you have it."

"I do?"

"But of course. Remember the fortnight I spent in Surrey with Elspeth James while her husband went haring off to attend to something or other at their estate in Scotland?"

Althea's eyes widened. "But Huggins took you and Colette there in the landau."

"And as soon as he departed, Marcus drove me to Dover, where he placed me in the capable hands of his associate, a Mr. John Soames, who saw to it that I got to Paris not too much the worse for wear. Elspeth is still under the illusion that Marcus and I are lovers."

"As is the rest of Society," Althea responded bitterly. "Mama, how could you sully your reputation for such a vain dream? Talleyrand would not risk so much as a broken fingernail to further your cause."

Althea was taken aback by the fierceness of her mother's response. "Pah! What do I care for the opinion of hypocrites?

I would gladly give my life for the merest chance to bring about the downfall of Napoleon Bonaparte."

"But why, Mama? Why? Surely that is a task better left to our armies?"

"Because I do not wish you, or any grandchildren you might give me, to suffer the horrors I experienced as a young girl."

Celeste looked inexpressibly sad.

Althea touched her arm. "I have never heard you mention it, but your flight to Calais with Uncle Jean-Claude must have been absolutely terrifying."

Celeste shrugged. "Oh, that? By then, I was too numb to feel anything. No. It was seeing my mother and father and my two brothers dragged away to their deaths by an angry mob."

Althea could not hold back her tears. "Mama, I had no idea."

"Nor did I intend that you should, but perhaps it is your right to know what can befall those in our position if we are not diligent."

"It is fortunate that our uncle was able to save you."

Celeste gave a dry laugh. "Come now, Althea, you should know better. It was my old nurse, Simone Boulanger, who saved me. She had long since been pensioned off, but when the angry peasants stormed our chateau in the middle of the night, she came directly to my chamber, stripped off a smock she was wearing, and put it on me."

Celeste was silent for a moment, then continued. "I could not even cry out when I heard my mother screaming as the mob dragged her away. Madame Boulanger held her hand over my face until I thought I should die of suffocation. Her hands smelled of garlic and the smock she put on me made my skin itch."

She stared at a bed of pansies as if lost in thought; then, to Althea's surprise, she looked up and smiled at her. "It is strange, is it not that of all the dreadful things that took place that night, the ones that stand out the clearest should be the smell of garlic and that itchy smock?"

Celeste wrinkled her nose. "To this day, I consider it a blessing that the English do not consider garlic to be quite the thing to put into their food."

"Mama, it is all so terribly sad. How was Uncle Jean-Claude able to find you?"

"That was not too difficult. The surprising thing was that he even took the trouble. His wife, our Aunt Marie, had recently died, and he came to visit us with the intention of leaving Cousin Gaston in our care."

Celeste plucked a blue Canterbury bell and without bothering to smell its fragrance, cast it to the ground. "When the peasants arrived, screaming for our blood, he grabbed Gaston and a small valise holding his valuables—I have no idea in which order—and escaped through a window on the ground floor and hid in the shrubbery."

"But how did he know where to find you—or even know that you had been spared, for that matter?"

"He saw Madame Boulanger and me leave. Uncle would not have recognized me if the shawl she gave me to cover my telltale red hair had not slipped. My head was exposed for but a moment, but a moment was all it took. He followed us to her cottage. Fortunately, the peasants were too busy robbing and vandalizing the chateau to notice."

"But bringing you to England was an added risk. Having a young girl along must have impeded his progress."

Celeste nodded. "Yes, it must have. But so did the valise full of valuables he carted with him, and in each case he considered it to be well worth the risk."

"Mama, what are you implying?"

"I am not implying anything, Althea. I thought I was making it perfectly clear. Uncle Jean-Claude brought me to England because he considered my looks sufficient to ensure me an advantageous match, thereby securing his own future."

Althea could not believe what she was hearing. "Mama, that is a dreadful thing to say. How could you malign him so?"

Celeste laughed. "Malign the Marquis de Maligny? Impossible!" Her mouth tightened. "I say it because it is true. When I refused to marry a dreadful old roué with whom he had negotiated for my hand, Uncle Jean-Claude berated me for not living up to my obligations."

Mortified, Althea cast a glance in Marcus's direction.

"Do not concern yourself with what I think, Althea," he inserted. "I consider your mother to be one of my closest friends, and as such, would never betray her confidence."

He gave her a wicked little smile. "Besides, it is not unusual for people of our class to enter into marriages of convenience."

"I think it is perfectly horrid."

"So do I."

Althea decided it was time to change the subject. "This Mr. Soames. Is he the same gentleman whom Mama sees fit to meet on the riverbank whenever the moon is full?"

"That is a slight exaggeration. Since your mother's meeting with Talleyrand, Mr. Soames has delivered but one package to Paris for her."

"And yet you see fit to have her embroiled in your intrigues?"

"Please, Althea," Celeste interjected. "Marcus allowed my participation only at my insistence. It has happened but twice, and on each occasion you managed to catch me." She shot Marcus a rueful look. "I doubt you will wish to continue with our arrangement."

Althea thought that Marcus responded with more amusement than displeasure. "Nonsense. At that time of night, most servants are sound asleep. If one of them should happen to see you haring off to the riverbank at such an ungodly hour, they would no doubt think you were trysting with a lover."

He turned to Althea. "I am sure that thought crossed your mind."

Althea felt her face flame. *How dare he presume such a thing.* "My mother has never given me reason to doubt her virtue," she replied coldly.

Marcus inclined his head. "My apologies, Althea. That was most indelicate of me. I did not mean to put your mother's honor to question. It is only that given the scene in question, my jaded view on life would lead me to jump to all sorts of reprehensible conclusions that probably would never occur to a virtuous young lady of your sensibility."

Althea had the grace to feel guilty. Had she not viewed her

mother's meeting with Mr. Soames with the same degree of cynicism as one of Society's biggest philanderers? Her claims to virtue and sensibility might be in doubt, but of one thing she was certain: no one could question the regrettable streak of hypocrisy she seemed to have acquired.

Althea addressed her next question to her mother. "How does this Mr. Soames know when to meet with you?"

"That is not too difficult. When Marcus is unable to keep their appointment at The Boar's Head, he knows to meet me at the river that night."

"I saw him signal you with a lantern the last time."

"That had nothing to do with Marcus. The previous month I had arranged for Mr. Soames to pick up a package from me on his return. His boat arrived a day early, that is all."

Althea was still not satisfied. "But Mama, surely you do not stay up every night on the off-chance that this Mr. Soames might show up."

Celeste laughed. "No, darling, I do not. With the aid of a spyglass, each boat can be clearly seen in the harbor at Camberly."

"Yes, I remember the spyglass. Papa and I used to watch the harbor with it. He would tell me what sort of boats were moored there, and what they were used for."

"The boat Mr. Soames sails on is called *The Seafoam* and is not very large, but carries sail on two masts and is a very graceful craft. It is designed for speed, not heavy cargo."

"My goodness, Mama. I have never known you to take an interest in such things."

Celeste wrinkled her nose. "Nor do I. On the trip across the channel, Mr. Soames conversed with me on a number of aspects of life at sea in a vain attempt to keep my mind off a dreadful attack of *mal-de-mer.*"

Althea patted her arm. "Poor Mama. You subject yourself to such indignities with so little return." She turned to Marcus. "Why, for instance, do you deem it necessary for my mother to 'hare' to the river, as you put it, in the middle of the night? Cannot this Mr. Soames call on Mama in a civilized manner to collect and deliver these messages that pass between you?"

Marcus nodded in Celeste's direction. "Because your mother wishes it."

Althea was perplexed. "Why, Mama? It does not make any sense."

Celeste set her jaw. "It makes perfectly good sense to me. I did not want Mr. Soames to be seen at the house. One cannot vouchsafe the loyalty of everyone under one's roof."

"But Mama, that is ridiculous. All the servants have been with us for years, most of them from families that have served at the Hall for many generations."

"Both our uncle and our cousin have valets who are French, as is my maid, Colette."

"But so are you, Mama, so how does that signify?"

"You should know better than to ask. England became my country the moment you were placed in my arms, *chérie*. Have you any idea how precious you were to me after losing my family to those bloodthirsty beasts? In any case, that is how I feel and Mr. Soames will just have to put up with it."

Althea stared at her mother in admiration. "Forgive me, darling, but all this time I have seen you as a frivolous creature with no more than the latest fashions on your mind, and now I have to adjust to you being a latter-day Boadicea, all girded to do battle with the enemy. It is a lot for me to take in all at once."

Chapter 8

It seemed to Althea that summer, with twilight lasting long after most people take to their beds, would never end. The restlessness of spirit that tormented her in the spring intensified as all of nature ripened, promising a bountiful harvest.

Each time she ventured into the village, whether to visit sick parishioners, call on the Swanns, or buy materials and trimmings at Hansford's, she always glanced in the direction of the pier, half hoping to see the young man again.

Althea acknowledged the foolishness of the exercise. Even if by some chance their paths did happen to cross once more, and that, wonder of wonders, he professed a *tendre* for her, nothing could come of it. Her duty to her family demanded that she marry a member of the *ton*, not a penniless adventurer who saw beauty in a dowdy governess.

One afternoon early in September, as Althea came in from the garden, she encountered her uncle at the foot of the grand staircase, making his final farewells to a pair of male visitors.

The taller of the two she recognized as a man he had presented to her and her mother the previous week as Monsieur Joubert. The man had dark, saturnine features and had subjected both ladies to a penetrating stare that Celeste had later confessed had sent a shiver down her spine. His companion, a Monsieur Delon, was, on the other hand, a plump and jovial individual with a receding thatch of straw-colored hair.

Both of them looked disheveled; their clothes, although of good quality, were sorely in need of a sponging and pressing, their linen long overdue for a change. Althea's nose also told her that it had been quite some time since either of them had seen fit to take a bath. In other words, not the sort of persons one would expect her uncle to honor with his gracious condescension, much less present to his niece as if they were her equals.

She took her leave of them as quickly as possible, seeking sanctuary in a small reception room. A cursory glance in a looking glass proved, as she had feared, her bonnet had not prevented the afternoon breeze from transforming the demure curls that framed her face into unruly disarray.

"It is all very well for Mama to say that such a style is becoming," she muttered. "The minute the wind rises, I look as though I have been dragged through the bushes."

She removed her bonnet and ran her fingers through the offending curls. They seemed to have a will of their own and would not be tamed. With a hopeless shrug, she cast her bonnet on a settee and slumped into a chair in a most unladylike manner.

She sat up straight immediately at the sound of a discreet knock on the door. It was her butler, Jarvis, a tall, portly individual whose pure white hair fringed his head like a monk's tonsure.

"Begging your pardon, my lady, but there is a Mr. Soames here to see you. He did not seem to be the sort of person you would wish to see, but he insists that he is here at your request."

Althea looked him squarely in the eye. "That is correct, Jarvis. Be so kind as to show the gentleman in."

The butler went to do her bidding, a pained expression on his face.

Althea wondered if her usually stony-faced retainer had yet to recover from the indignity of having to admit the previous visitors into his hallowed domain. Surely, she thought, Marcus Ridley would not have entrusted her mother into the care of someone equally as disreputable.

Althea was still pondering this question when John Soames was ushered into her presence. Althea rose to her feet and stood stock-still as he made his bow. Without a word, she signaled for Jarvis to leave the room.

Once they were alone, Althea sat down and invited her visitor to do likewise. Mr. Soames complied, choosing a chair directly facing hers.

Althea made the opening remark. "It seems that we meet

again, Mr. Soames."

He looked puzzled, then said, "I am afraid you have the advantage of me, madam."

Althea suffered a stab of disappointment. Evidently she had not made a lasting impression on the young man. Then she remembered that her appearance had drastically altered since the afternoon they had met on the pier.

She was about to refresh his memory when he said, "Ah yes, I recognize your voice. Tell me, madam, are you in the habit of pretending to be a dowdy little governess, or was that shoddy little masquerade staged for my benefit?"

No longer in shock, Althea felt her anger rising. "Sir, you delude yourself. At the time we met, I did not even know of your existence. Besides, I did not say I was a governess. You took it upon yourself to presume such, and, I might add, I did not find it at all flattering."

Althea thought her outburst would elicit an apology from him but instead he gave a short laugh and said, "That would explain why you gave that dreadful coat to one of your servants. Your abigail, most likely. Please extend my apologies. I saw her wearing it along the esplanade and, thinking it was you, ran to catch up with her. She turned around, took one look at me, then turned tail and scurried away like a frightened fox with a pack of hounds in hot pursuit."

Althea doubted that John Soames had ever been accused of being tactful, but found it hard not to laugh at his story. Then a disquieting thought entered her mind. In Lizzie's place, would she have waited for him to catch up with her? Her musings came to an end with his next remark.

"You should laugh more often. It crinkles up your face in a most beguiling manner."

Althea felt an unfamiliar glow of elation, which she instantly quenched. "I beg your pardon?"

He looked rueful. "Forgive me for the impertinence. It may be selfish of me, but in a way I wish you really were a governess, and not a great lady."

"Oh? What possible difference could it make to you,

Mr. Soames?"

"It could have changed both our lives. You see, my lady, ever since I met her, I have been unable to get a proper little governess with the most enchanting eyes I have ever beheld out of my mind, and now I discover that some fairy has waved a magic wand and played a cruel trick."

"A cruel trick?" Althea echoed, preparing to put an end to his nonsense.

"Yes," he said solemnly. "The cruelest one a fay could ever devise. She made my governess even more beautiful and then, to punish me for daring to dream, turned her into this rich and powerful lady. Forgive me if I mourn my loss."

Althea forced a smile. "Really? I rather suspect that your governess would be far too sensible to believe such a tarradiddle."

He returned her smile, resulting in a flash of white teeth and a heart-lurching display of dimples. The smile faded and the gray of his eyes darkened. Althea was lost in their depths for several moments before she came to her senses. *His fairy is working her magic on me,* she thought, and immediately broke eye contact with him.

She cleared her throat. "To be quite frank, Mr. Soames, I am surprised you called on me. I rather hoped that your, er, associate would see fit to dispense with my mother's services."

"As long as Lady Camberly wishes to assist us, neither Lord Ridley nor myself has the heart to deny her."

"Deny her?"

"You do not know the lady very well, even if she is your mother—or perhaps it is because she *is* your mother that you do not."

"I beg your pardon?"

"You are not alone in this. Most of us do not really know our parents because of the role they play in our lives. We are all inclined to see Mama and Papa as extensions of the holy family and refuse to acknowledge that our existence stems from a passion they share, or just like us, that they harbor within them, a wellspring of hopes and dreams."

As he spoke, Althea perceived that his face had taken on an

intensity that bespoke a great capacity for passion of his own. His words hit an uncomfortable chord.

"Mr. Soames, I do not think this conversation is quite the thing. Besides, I fail to see how it has any bearing on the subject. My mother is merely exchanging packages with you on the banks of the Camber at a time better spent getting a good night's sleep."

Althea was taken aback by his reaction.

"And Joan of Arc was a hysterical young woman who should have been locked up in an asylum, not put at the head of an army." He threw up his hands. *"Brava,* Lady Camberly, spoken like a good little member of the flock. Convince your mother that what she does is of little importance, and perhaps you can get her to return to the fold. No doubt it would make your life a lot less complicated. But what would it do to her?"

Althea opened her mouth to object, but the words would not form.

He softened his tone. "Forgive me, Lady Camberly. I am well aware that any number of people could perform the service your mother renders. But put yourself in her place. She saw her family dragged to their deaths, and was powerless to help them." He leaned forward. "As she was powerless to help herself. The Marquis de Maligny gave her very little say in how her life should be run."

"You seem to have taken it upon yourself to delve into things that are none of your concern, Mr. Soames."

"I would not presume to do such. During our stay in France, your mother and I confided in one another about many things. Barriers are lowered when two people share the privations of such a journey."

He held out his hands as if in supplication. "All Lady Camberly wants is to ensure that you are never put in the same situation. To this end she is willing to do anything, however insignificant. Do you not see? By this 'exchanging of packages,' as you put it, your mother has finally gained some control over her own destiny."

"A trifle colorful, Mr. Soames, but what you say has some

merit and I thank you for championing my mother's cause. I make but one request."

"Yes?"

"I ask that in future, you meet with her under this roof at a reasonable hour of the day."

He smiled ruefully. "I would gladly comply, but alas, I doubt the lady will agree. As it is, she will not be at all happy to hear of my coming here this afternoon."

"No, I expect not."

Mr. Soames stood up. "Lady Camberly, it was most kind of you to receive me and I hope you forgive my frankness in championing your mother's cause in this matter. Over the past year I have grown to harbor a great respect and regard for her and would not like to see her deprived of her *raison d'être*. I fear it would be most detrimental for her well-being."

Althea stood up also. "I quite agree, although I confess to having misgivings over the matter."

"It is only natural. It is hardly the sort of pastime one would wish for one's mother. But rest assured, she will come to no harm."

"I fervently hope so. Before you go, Mr. Soames, please allow me to offer you some refreshment. I fully intended to when my butler first announced you, but with the rather unsettling circumstances that followed, I quite forgot."

He inclined his head. "It is most kind of you, madam, but I must decline. I partook of a meal at the inn in Camberly before coming here."

"Then I shall detain you no further, Mr. Soames." Althea offered him her hand and immediately regretted it. She was not in the habit of conferring such intimacy on strange gentlemen. She was not so sure that John Soames should even be considered as such.

He did not take her hand right away, but stared at her for a moment, a quizzical expression on his face. Althea was tempted to pull her hand back, but too late, he took it, scarcely touching more than her gloved fingertips, and gave it a brief shake.

At his touch a strange sensation coursed through Althea

and her heartbeat quickened to an alarming rate. It was as if a swarm of butterflies was trapped within her body, desperately trying to get out. With great effort she regained her composure enough to say, "Good afternoon, Mr. Soames. It was good of you to call."

"No. This is good-bye," he replied, and searched her face as if committing it to memory. "For I doubt we shall have occasion to meet again."

Althea thought there was a note of regret in his voice. His words filled her with a terrible sense of loss. She wanted to grab the sleeve of his jacket and prevent him from leaving. Instead she inclined her head when he took his leave, then clutched her throat when his footsteps echoed on the marble floor as he made his way down the front hall to the great double doors at the entrance.

When she heard the sound of his horse's hooves clopping down the tree-lined approach to the house, she rushed to the window and watched his departure. He turned his head once, then urged the horse to a faster pace. It struck her that the horse, a handsome roan, was too fine an animal to have been hired from The Boar's Head, and wondered how he came by such a mount. She decided that the animal probably came from Marcus Ridley's stables and most likely was boarded at the inn.

John made his departure from Camberly Hall, filled with despair. Ever since he met Althea Markham on the pier he had harbored a longing to see her again and hoped that one day he might be allowed to know her better.

He had admired her odd mixture of quiet modesty and haughty pride. Her pale green eyes bespoke an affinity for a sylvan deity. A passionate nature latent in the coolness of their depths. *That's it*, he thought. *She is an odd mixture of fire and water. Everything about her is a paradox. I doubt few men could understand her and even fewer could appreciate what a marvelous creature she is.*

Until that afternoon it was bad enough that he harbored a *tendre* for a young woman he had met but once and was not likely to see again. There was always the possibility that their paths might cross in the future.

To this end, on his visits to Camberly, he had spent an inordinate amount of time leaning against the rails of the pier, his eyes focused on the large house he had seen her enter. But she never crossed the threshold.

Once, he saw an older woman leave the house with several boys in tow and resigned himself to the possibility that the young woman had sought employment elsewhere. He even determined that when control of his life was restored to him, he would make inquiries as to her whereabouts. It was not much but it gave him some hope to cling to.

He turned his head for one last glimpse of Camberly Hall, and thought he saw a curtain move. "You need not worry, my fine lady. I shall bother you no more with my foolish ravings," he muttered.

He straightened in the saddle and applied a slight pressure to his mount's flanks with his knees. "Come on, Orion, you can move faster than that." Once out of the gates of Camberly Hall, he headed in the direction of Brighton, where he picked up the London Road and rode north. With a stopover at Fairfax Towers in Surrey, the countryseat of his parents, he expected to join his brother in London the following morning.

On the way, he had plenty of time to go over his encounter with the Countess of Camberly. He winced when he recalled the way he had spoken to her. As if babbling on about fairies and magic wands was not bad enough, what on earth inspired him to spend the rest of the time pontificating about how she should treat her mother?

"Oh, what difference does it make? I could be the most perspicacious fellow in England, for all the good it would do me. High-in-the-instep countesses do not marry second sons and that's that."

As if in response to his outburst, Orion gave a startled whinny.

For a brief moment John wondered if it would have helped his suit with Althea Markham if he had been born first and had his brother's expectations. He immediately dismissed this line of thinking as ignoble.

The following evening after dinner, while enjoying a glass of the cognac with Marcus that he smuggled in from France from time to time, he confided his plight.

"For goodness' sake, tell the girl how you feel."

John scowled. "Really, Marcus, I sometimes wonder if you are in complete possession of your faculties. I should imagine that if a rough fellow like John Soames had the effrontery to plead his suit to such a highborn lady, she would have the dogs set on him for his pains."

Marcus laughed. "I am sure Althea would turn such a fellow down out of hand—but set the dogs on him? I hardly think so. She is far too nice a person for that. But she might be receptive to John Ridley. You do quite nicely once you take a bath and put on some decent clothes."

"You will forgive me for disagreeing with you, but apart from being the better for a little sprucing up, there is nothing else to commend me."

Marcus pushed his shoulder. "Enough of that defeatism. What have you got to lose?"

"I fail to see where all this is leading."

"Do not be so obtuse. If you ask the lady for her hand, what is the worst thing that can happen?"

John frowned. "She could say no, for starters."

"Yes, she could. But she could also say yes."

"That is hardly likely."

"I quite agree. But if you do not ask, you will never know. In other words, brother, you have nothing to lose by trying."

"I suppose not. Perhaps when this ridiculous masquerade is over, I shall try, in which case it behooves me to lay in considerably more of this cognac. I would have to be foxed for a week before even considering it."

"In which case, it would take another week for you to learn what her answer was."

John laughed.

"That's better, John. That is the first time I have seen

you laugh since you got here. It won't do, you know. No girl is worth that."

John gazed thoughtfully at his brother. "You have never been in love, have you?"

"One or two have set my blood boiling. But not the sort of girl one marries, of course. But love? I expect not. Otherwise, I probably would have been leg-shackled long before now."

As John lay in his chamber that night, waiting for sleep to give him respite from his misery, he envied Marcus's seeming immunity to Cupid's darts.

Chapter 9

The arrival of autumn at Camberly was almost imperceptible, the weather in the early days of October varying little from that of September. Then one night, the frost turned the dew to crystals and the leaves upon the trees began to turn.

The following morning, Althea and Celeste strolled through the gardens, noticing the changes one night of cold had managed to bring about. Celeste plucked a wilted peony. "Even though I know it is inevitable, the passing of summer always fills me with sadness. It is like mourning the death of a friend."

Althea looked askance; she could never understand her mother's expenditure of emotion over what she deemed the most mundane of occurrences. "Come now, Mama. That is a trifle extreme. Summer will return next year. Alas, the same cannot be said of departed loved ones."

Celeste tapped her on the shoulder with the flower. *'La,* child. Must you always persist in being so single-mindedly *English?* It can be very tiresome."

Althea smiled. *How could two people from the same family differ so? I love Mama, but I fear I could never understand her.*

Celeste chose that moment to venture off the path to take a closer look at a grouping of mature horse chestnut trees. Noticing how the ground pushed up around the trunks, Althea opened her mouth with the intention of warning her to watch her step, but was too late. With a startled cry, Celeste went sprawling on the grass.

With little heed for her own advice, Althea rushed to her side. Celeste raised her head and gave Althea a rueful look. "That was foolish of me, I must say."

She held out her hand for Althea to assist her to her feet,

but with a tiny moan, sank back. "It is no use—I think I might have sprained my ankle. You had better go for help."

Althea dashed across the lawn and bounded up to the front of Camberly Hall. She tried to take the huge granite steps two at a time, but tripped and landed on her knees.

A young footman, standing on duty in the Hall, happened to be gazing through the window at the time and dashed outside to help her. But she waved him away and struggled to her feet.

"Pray do not waste time with me. My mother is hurt. She is over by the horse chestnut trees. Please, hurry."

The young man dashed off and Althea went into the hall and pointed to another footman. "What are you waiting for? Go and help. Hurry. Come on now, for goodness' sake, *hurry.*"

Jarvis bustled into the hall. "Is something amiss, madam?"

"Ah, Jarvis. Will you please send for Doctor Hervey? Lady Camberly tripped over a tree root and, I fear, has sustained an injury to her foot."

By the time the groom had ridden into Camberly and found the doctor, helped saddle his horse, and escorted him back, the better part of an hour had elapsed. By then, Celeste's usually shapely ankle had swollen and she was in considerable pain.

Doctor Hervey was in his forties, with wispy gray hair and a pale, delicate-looking face. His inspection of Celeste's ankle involved a lot of palping and squeezing on his part.

"There is no cause for concern—the ankle is merely sprained," he said. He proceeded to apply a poultice to the injury and secured it with a firmly tied bandage. "I would strongly recommend the application of leeches, but I know that madam has no love for the treatment."

"Absolutely not. I consider it a barbaric and disgusting practice. I would rather die than submit to it."

The doctor steepled his fingers. "I am unhappy to say that there may come a time, your ladyship, that such may be the case."

After he left, Celeste had Colette remove the bandages, take off the poultice, and rewrap her injured ankle in a dry bandage.

"What on earth good will soggy bread wrapped in a rag do for anything? The man is a charlatan."

She then submitted to the inevitable and sat facing the window with her foot propped up on a footstool. When Althea dropped in to check on her condition, she found her gazing outside, an exasperated expression on her face.

Althea hastened to her side and brushed a kiss on her cheek. "Oh, dear. You look absolutely miserable. Would you like something to ease the pain?"

"Nonsense, darling. As long as I do not move my foot too much, it feels perfectly fine."

This statement was followed by a speculative look. Althea knew it did not—nay, could not—bode well for her.

"There *is* something that you could do for me, darling. Heaven knows I hate to impose, but I must prevail upon you to perform a trifling little service for me. In fact, I must *insist* that you do it."

"What would that be, Mama?"

"Marcus called on me yesterday while you were out delivering baskets to the old and infirm of the village."

"And he left you a letter to give to Mr. Soames."

"Yes. But how did you know that?"

"Difficult to say. It just popped right into my head. It could have something to do with there being a full moon tonight. For some reason, your rendezvous with Mr. Soames and the existence of a full moon seem to go hand in hand."

Celeste beamed, "Then you will deliver it for me, *chérie?*"

Althea nodded, surprised that her usually astute mother did not catch the irony in her response. "When do you expect to meet him?"

"About ten o'clock tonight. It should be dark enough by then."

"Yes, it should, but the servants will still be up. Uncle Jean-Claude will most likely not even have finished his after-dinner brandy and cigars."

Celeste huffed impatiently. "For goodness' sake, Althea, pray do not make more of this than is necessary. Is not the lady of the house entitled to take a walk in the garden when she pleases? If you tippy-toe out, casting furtive glances right and left, of course you will be suspect. March through the front door as bold as you please and no one will give it a second thought."

Althea had to admit that Celeste's view on the subject had merit. "That is very clever of you, Mama."

Celeste waived the compliment. "Nonsense. It is merely common sense."

Clad in a warm coat made of a pale blue superfine and wearing a silk bonnet of the same color, Althea walked—nay, strode—through the front door, nodding at every servant she encountered along the way.

From the moment she agreed to meet John Soames, a feeling of panic robbed her of all logical thought The memory of their last encounter was all too vivid. The slightest hint of a smile on his part had made her senses reel, and the sound of his voice had washed over her like a caress. She had thought her body had betrayed her in every way it could, but that was before he had taken her hand in his...

"Dear heavens," she moaned, "do not let it happen again."

Even as she uttered the supplication, she peered into the looking glass to make sure that her bonnet was placed at a becoming angle and that she looked her prettiest. She mulled over these contradictions as she made her way to the river, firmly convinced that she was quite mad.

As she neared the bridle path, John came forward to meet her. "Lady Camberly," he called out when they were but a few feet apart, "how pleasant it is to see you once mo—"

He stood stock-still. "I seem to have my Lady Camberlys mixed up, but the greeting still applies."

"How good of you," Althea replied dryly.

"How is the older Lady Camberly—not ill, I hope?"

"Not exactly. She tripped over a tree root this morning and twisted her ankle. Nothing serious, but the doctor recommends that she stay off her foot for a while."

"I see."

John took a step nearer. Her bonnet shadowed her eyes,

making it impossible for him to see her expression. He took another step. The moonlight gave her face a luminous quality that took his breath away. *Steady, old chap. It will not do to overstep the bounds.*

Not trusting his emotions, John came no farther and to his dismay, Althea came to him, holding out a package.

"Mama asked me to give you this."

Her voice was high-pitched and strained. John concluded that Althea was uncomfortable with the idea of meeting a comparative stranger in the middle of the night without a chaperone, and rightly so. He made up his mind to be scrupulous in observing the conventions.

He took the package and put it in his jacket pocket, telling himself that he would thank her and be on his way.

To his dismay she tilted her face up to his and parted her lips as if to say something. Helpless to resist, he pulled her close and kissed her.

At first, her body stiffened and her lips clamped shut; then, with a soft moan, she parted them and received his kiss. He claimed their softness with gentle probings and tiny nips, taking care not to frighten her, and to his infinite joy, he felt her arms slowly entwine his neck.

Emboldened, he showered her face and throat with kisses; then, no longer able to contain his desire for her, his lips joined hers in an ever-deepening kiss. John had never felt so right about kissing a girl in his life. Although kissing Althea raised him to the heights of passion, it also filled him with a sense of belonging.

At first he found this difficult to fathom; then he realized it was a sense of recognition. It was as if he had known her from the beginning of time and would continue to do so long after the stars grew cold.

"Dear girl. You have no idea how long I have wanted to kiss you, and to hold you close like this."

He took her hand and held it to his chest. "Feel my heart—it is beating so rapidly it is liable to burst."

She pulled her hand away and he reclaimed it and kissed the back of it, then unfolded her fingers like the petals of a flower and kissed each fingertip.

"We belong together. I have never been so sure of anything in my life."

Her reaction to his declaration was like a dash of cold water in his face. She freed herself from his embrace and pushed him away.

"This cannot go further. I am sorry, Mr. Soames, but my life is not my own."

John drew back. "My name is John." He fought to keep his voice from breaking. "You cannot kiss a man the way you kissed me, and then treat him like a stranger."

"John, then. But it doesn't change the situation." Her face crumpled with distress. "Oh dear, I cannot be a party to this. I am sorry, but I have to go."

Before John could say anything to stop her, she took flight down the path that led to Camberly Hall. As he watched her disappear into the shadows, he felt as if everything important to his existence had disappeared with her.

It seemed to him that in her way, Althea Markham was no better than Belinda Vickery. Perhaps all women were alike. When it came right down to it, most marriages of the *ton* were based on wealth and rank rather than love.

"I fear that love carries no significance for you, Lady Camberly—or could it be that it is not in your nature to love any man?"

He turned to the river, realizing that it made no difference. No matter what qualities Althea Markham did, or did not, possess, he was doomed to love her until the day he died.

Chapter 10

Althea spent the winter months in a state of abject misery. She longed to search out John Soames and tell him she had made a terrible mistake and ask him to forgive her, but she knew that was out of the question. Circumstances had not changed. She could not marry him. Besides, *The Seafoam* never returned to Camberly.

In January, King George slipped deeper into insanity, and the Prince of Wales assumed the title of Prince Regent. Despite the cold weather, the inhabitants of Camberly gathered together in groups along the esplanade for the next couple of weeks speculating how much money their Prince Regent planned to squander on remodeling his pavilion in Brighton.

During February of 1811, an epidemic of the grippe swept through Camberly, leaving several deaths in its wake. Those who died were mostly very old, but two small children also succumbed, causing Althea to feel shame for having wallowed in self-pity since that night in October.

One of the people who had died was a Mrs. John Underhill, the sister of the Countess of Fairfax and aunt to Marcus and John Ridley. She lived in a large house on a cliff overlooking the ocean, just beyond the boundaries of the village.

The house was rectangular in design, built of large blocks of gray stone. An imposing-looking portico comprised of half a dozen Corinthian pillars relieved the austerity of its form.

Althea had always admired the simplicity of its style. She saw in it a harmony lacking in the jumble of towers and crennelations of Camberly Hall. She felt it was a house that cried out to be filled with children, its sturdy walls promising a safe haven against the winter storms that roiled the ocean below.

John Underhill had built the house in 1769, prior to his marriage to Gertrude Wilson, with every expectation of rearing a large family there. Unfortunately, children were not forthcoming.

The Underhills were a reclusive couple, not given to socializing with their neighbors. Even in church, they would merely nod to the Markhams, then keep their eyes steadfastly fixed on the altar.

Althea and Celeste had become better acquainted with Mrs. Underhill almost three years ago when, out of respect, they attended her husband's funeral. The Earl and Countess of Fairfax had been there, along with their son, the Viscount Ridley. The younger son, John, did not attend because he was in Jamaica, seeing to the family sugar plantation.

Lady Fairfax, it turned out, was Mrs. Underhill's younger sister. Celeste thought it odd that Mrs. Underhill had not made use of such a lofty connection to secure her place in Society. She received the answer when Marcus asked her and Althea to befriend his aunt.

"We would be delighted to do so," Celeste replied, "but I doubt your aunt would welcome any attempt at friendship on our part. When my husband was alive, all invitations to attend our soirees were politely but firmly refused by the Underhills."

"Do not blame my aunt. Mr. Underhill was a kind, decent man but was terribly shy, and did not seek the society of others. It must not have been easy for Aunt Gertrude as the Wilsons are a jolly, fun-loving family."

Once, at a picnic Althea gave by the River Camber, she sat next to Mrs. Underhill and together they watched the Swann boys chasing a ball all over the meadow, a large, shaggy dog of indeterminate pedigree clashing among them, barking with sheer joy.

After an interval Mrs. Underhill said, "I do not know how Mrs. Swann keeps up with such a brood. Mr. Underhill and I had hoped to raise a family, but fate decreed otherwise."

Althea touched her hand lightly. "How sad for you, Mrs. Underhill."

Mrs. Underhill looked away from the children and gave

Althea a smile. "*La,* my dear Lady Camberly, I have come to the conclusion that as far as the little darlings are concerned, I have none to make me laugh and none to make me cry." But even as she uttered the words, Althea had seen the hint in her eyes.

On hearing of Mrs. Underbill's demise, Althea recalled her words and was filled with profound sadness.

Due to the fact that all four of them were suffering from one stage of the grippe or another, none of the residents of Camberly Hall were able to attend Mrs. Underbill's funeral. Althea regretted this, and sent her condolences to Lord and Lady Fairfax and also to Marcus Ridley.

In the middle of March, Celeste paid a visit to Hansford's to purchase some thread and lace trimmings to refurbish some of her underclothes in readiness for the upcoming Season. Althea had declined to accompany her to the village, using the excuse that she had no intention of participating in the social round that year.

"You must go to Town without me, Mama. I am of the opinion that four Seasons should be enough for any female to find a husband. If a young gentleman wishes to pay me court, he shall have to come to Camberly to do so."

"But Althea, this could prove to be a brilliant Season for you. You will have the cream of society's eligibles at your feet, all *dying* to marry you."

"And also Society's most dreadful bounders. Married persons hoping to seduce me into tossing my bonnet over the windmill. Thank you, but no, Mama. I would far rather stay at Camberly."

On her return from the village, Celeste sought Althea out to share the latest *on dits* circulating there.

"Darling, whom do you think I encountered at Hansford's?"

"I would not venture a guess."

"Mary Swann."

"Oh, dear. How is she? I have been meaning to call on her, but what with catching the grippe last month…" Althea's voice trailed off. It was a poor excuse. She had begun neglecting her social obligations from the time she had rejected John Soames's offer of love.

"She is in the very bloom of health and in the family way once more. Mary is one of those fortunate females who seem to thrive at such times."

"That *is* good news. Perhaps she will get the little girl she has always hoped for."

"That would be nice. She also told me that Mrs. Underhill bequeathed her entire fortune to her nephew, John Ridley."

"John Ridley? That would have to be Marcus's younger brother. I find it most singular that after four years of being out in Society I have yet to encounter him. Have you, Mama?"

"No, *chérie*, but it has been years since anyone has. I rather suspect that he is an eccentric."

"You mean he hides himself away like a hermit?"

Celeste laughed. "Nothing quite so drastic. According to Marcus, he managed the family's sugar interests in Jamaica for a while. While there, he also became engaged to a beautiful young woman who subsequently jilted him for someone with fuller pockets. Not long after, he left the island."

"She must have been a very shallow creature, do you not agree?"

Celeste sighed. "Yes, darling, I do. But there are many in Society who would choose riches over love. Some manage to rub along quite well with their spouses, but there are others…" She did not finish the sentence.

Althea wished she had not pursued the subject. Had not her mother entered into such an arrangement? Admittedly she had been under tremendous pressure to contract an advantageous union but had refused out of hand to marry the first two candidates presented to her.

Not long after the earl died, Celeste had told Althea that she had consented to marry her father because he was the only decent man the marquis had presented to her.

"There was not a grand passion between us. I am sure Papa experienced such in his youth, but what we shared was an affection that comes with mutual regard and consideration."

"What became of John Ridley?"

"According to Marcus, he dashed off to India to explore ancient temples. Such an odd thing for a young man to do. Do you not agree?"

"Foreign climes seem to hold a fascination for several gentlemen of our acquaintance."

"Quite. But they are those more settled in life. The sort who seek to escape the monotony of a long-standing marriage. On the other hand, most twenty-three-year-old gentlemen are more inclined to move among Society, gaming and cavorting with *belles amies,* while at the same time, halfheartedly searching for an heiress to marry who is not an out-and-out antidote. But, of course, that would not be the case here. The poor man is probably trying to mend a broken heart."

"Mama, I am so afraid it will happen to me."

"A broken heart?"

"No. That someone will pretend to love me just for my fortune. It is all so odious. Mama, why is it that the families of the *ton* see nothing wrong in marrying their daughters off to such creatures, providing they have the right pedigrees?"

Celeste looked wry. *"La,* child, whom should our kind choose for their daughters to marry? Poor but saintly creatures who will worship and adore them in squalid little hovels for the rest of their days? Is that the sort of life you would choose for yourself?"

"Of course not, Mama. Only I think it would be better if the *ton* raised their children to believe that they should cherish love and honor far above their pedigrees."

"But darling, young men defend their honor on the grass at dawn all the time."

Althea frowned. "Do not deliberately misunderstand me, Mama. Those silly little duels have more to do with fools drinking too much wine the previous evening than ever they have with honor."

"I quite agree," Celeste said quietly. "Just as this conversation has very little to do with the marriage customs of Society. *Chérie,* until you tell me what is making you so unhappy, there is nothing I can do to help."

Althea forced a smile. "You are mistaken, Mama. I am quite happy. I must admit that I am still a trifle weak from the grippe. But I am sure that when the weather improves, I shall feel better."

Celeste patted her cheek. "Of course you will. Just remember that you can come to me for any reason at any time, day or night."

Althea made no reply.

On first learning that his niece was not planning on a season in London, the Marquis de Maligny seemed disappointed, and questioned the wisdom of such a step. Althea suspected that his objections were colored more by a fear that her absence from the social round would result in fewer invitations for him to participate in the Season's festivities, rather than any concern for her welfare.

A day or so later, he completely reversed his stand on the subject. At the time, she was taking her morning walk in the garden when she heard the sound of someone scurrying along the gravel path behind her. Thinking the head gardener wished to consult her on her choice of summer blooms, she turned and discovered it was her uncle making a laborious approach.

On reaching her, he took out a handkerchief and wiped his brow. "Must you walk so fast, child?" He wheezed, his breath coming in painful gasps. "It is unbecoming of you to take such mannish strides."

Althea responded by continuing her walk. The marquis matched steps with her. She was tempted to walk faster, but her better nature prevailing, she slowed her pace and inquired of him how she could be of service.

"I seek nothing for myself, my dear," he gushed. "I am concerned only for your happiness."

Althea braced herself for what was to follow, knowing from experience that when the marquis adapted such a selfless stance it was usually a preliminary to instill within her sufficient guilt to satisfy his most outrageous demands.

"My dear niece, after careful consideration I have decided that you are wise to forgo the London Season."

"Oh?" His remark irked her. Something contrary in her nature tempted her to change her mind about staying in the country.

He wiped his brow once more and nodded toward a bench. "I must prevail upon you to sit down. This sort of exertion is apt to upset my liver."

Althea complied, carefully arranging the folds of her pelisse so as not to wrinkle it. The marquis sat down beside her, his joints creaking as he did so. Althea regarded him with sympathy. It seemed that in the past year, old age had caught up with him, draining him of his last vestige of manly vigor.

"Ah, that is better. This dreadful damp air seeps right through my bones. Er—as I was saying, I see nothing wrong with staying at Camberly. A young lady is not safe these days. I saw those two blackguards making indecent overtures towards you at the prince's soiree last summer. I was sorely tempted to call them out over it, but considering where we were, I did not think it would be quite the thing."

Althea gave him a wry smile. "I quite agree, Uncle Jean-Claude. It was most circumspect of you."

"Beautiful young maidens are always at the mercy of such villains—that is why I took care to see that our dear Celeste was safely married as soon as possible when we came to this country."

Althea could see where the conversation was leading and found it most disquieting. Surely the man did not have the temerity to think that he could dispose of her in like manner?

"Althea, my dear, I want you to consider what I am about to suggest most carefully before coming to a decision on the matter."

Althea made to rise, but he stayed her with his hand. "Please stay."

Althea settled back. "Very well. But be assured I do not intend to marry just to fend off would-be seducers. Besides, from my observations, a wedding ring does not deter such predators. Quite the opposite."

"Of course I would not suggest that you marry for such a reason. I merely brought up the subject to point out the advantages of marriage to someone whose love and respect you already have."

"And who might that be?"

"Our dear Philippe."

Chapter 11

Althea's jaw dropped on hearing her great-uncle's choice of husband for her. *Good heavens, how does one respond to such a proposition? There is not a tactful way to tell an old gentleman that his grandson just will not do.*

An awful thought came to her. *What if Uncle Jean-Claude has already discussed this matter with Philippe and he has agreed to this marriage? I love him too much to want to hurt him. He is a good and honorable young man.*

"Tell me, Uncle, have you spoken to Philippe about this?"

"Of course not. I would not presume to do so until I knew his suit would be well received. For a young man, he has very delicate sensibilities."

Althea felt a weight lift from her shoulders. *Thank goodness for doting grandfathers!*

"Uncle, I am honored that you would consider me a worthy match for Philippe. I know he is the apple of your eye, and with good reason. He is indeed a fine young main, but I must insist that you give me time to think the matter over. I fear I see Philippe more as a brother than a suitor. The idea might take quite a bit of getting used to."

The marquis patted her shoulder. "Splendid. By all means, consider the matter. You are a sensible girl and I am sure you will make the right decision. As you so wisely pointed out, Philippe is a fine young man." He looked arch. "And handsome, too, I might add."

"I agree, Uncle. Our Philippe is one of the handsomer young gentlemen of our acquaintance."

Once Althea was in the privacy of her own chambers, she delved more deeply into the matter. Philippe was indeed a very handsome young man and yes, they both held a fond regard for one another… Try as she may, Althea could not visualize sharing passionate kisses with him. John Soames would creep into her thoughts and take his place.

At least once a week, the marquis would arrange to get her alone, then with raised brow would say, "Well? Have you decided?"

She would respond, "I have to consider the matter further. Marriage is a very serious step." This tactic proved to be very successful, for they were well into May without her having to give him an answer.

In the meantime, she made a conscious effort to better understand the inner workings of Philippe's mind. He was skilled in the social chatter that passed for conversation at most "at homes." In fact, his flair for saying nothing in the most amusing manner possible made him the darling of Society's hostesses.

Quite a few young ladies, with or without the encouragement of their mamas, had tried to inveigle him into a courtship, to no avail. The young ladies were usually captivated by his easy charm and handsome features; their mamas, on the other hand, took an avid interest in his impending barony and the fortune that went with it.

Philippe was known to venture an opinion on the performance of an opera or a play now and then, but Althea had no idea what he thought about the politics of the day, or even if he cared as to the outcome of the war being waged against France. She liked to think that Philippe's reticence in voicing his opinions was due to an innate shyness rather than consider the possibility that he might not have any.

After one fruitless afternoon of trying to break through the barrier that Philippe seemed to hide behind, Althea was sorely tempted to shake him until his thoughts came tumbling out. Instead, she excused herself and sought refuge in her chambers.

With the door firmly closed, she clenched her fists and shook from head to toe with frustration. "Aargh!" she cried. "I have known Philippe all of my life, yet he is still not comfortable enough to share even his most inconsequential thoughts with me.

Uncle will have to find another bride for his precious lambkin."

During the following week, Althea was relieved that the marquis did not once bring up the subject. Wishing to postpone an awkward confrontation as long as possible, she did her best to stay out of his way. Then one day, a trip she made to Hansford's shop changed everything.

As she was leaving, she came face-to-face with John Soames. She handed her purchases to Lizzie and was about to take her place in the trap when she was stayed by his voice.

"Please, Lady Camberly. Do not go until you hear what I have to say."

She faced him and was shocked by the misery she saw in his eyes. Her instincts told her to get into the trap and depart with all speed, but she could not do it.

"Very well." She turned to Lizzie, who was sitting on the passenger side of the conveyance, her eyes wide and questioning. "This will take but a moment."

John gestured for them to move further up the esplanade, and not wishing her abigail to overhear their conversation, she complied.

Althea spoke first. "Mr. Soames, there is no point to this."

"No point?" His voice was bitter. "Only if you consider the happiness of two people of little significance. Great heavens, woman, I love you, and your kisses tell me that you love me, too."

Even in her distress, the thought crossed Althea's mind that it was not exactly the most elegant declaration of love a lady could receive. John Soames was definitely not the sort of person who dazzles the *ton* with his wit and *éclat*. But neither was she.

Althea forced herself to sound indifferent. "Please do not place so much importance on a few harmless kisses."

"Althea, reject my suit if you must, but do not lie to me."

She touched his sleeve, and noticed it had a slight tear in it. He was sorely in need of a woman's care.

"No, Mr. Soames, I will not lie to you."

"Call me John. I should like to hear my name on your lips one more time."

"Very well—John. I cannot deny that when you kissed me I

felt—something. I also will admit to thinking of you with some affection, but this is not reason enough to forget my duty to my family. There can be nothing more between us."

"But my dear girl, there is nothing to stop us from marrying. I am not a pauper. Leave Camberly Hall to the others in your family. Marry me and live under my roof. I promise to take good care of you."

Althea was touched by his words. She looked at the condition of his clothes. Effigies of Guy Fawkes were burned on bonfires wearing better on any fifth of November.

"Dear, dear sir, I am sure that you would care for me to the utmost of your ability, but I am promised to another."

He bowed to her, his lips compressed into a tight line. "My apologies. Had there been talk of it in the village, I would not have importuned you thus. May I ask when this marriage is to take place?"

Althea's heart sank. She had been treed by a falsehood blurted out on the spur of the moment. When should she say the marriage is to take place?

She looked into his fine gray eyes, filled with both love and suffering, and she felt herself melting.

"The last Saturday of the month."

It was an act of desperation. If she waited too long to marry Philippe, she knew there was a good chance she would be scouring Camberly in search of John.

"I think you will find, Althea, that a marriage of convenience is anything but. It is my sincere wish, my dear, that yours proves to be the exception." With those words, he turned on his heel and strode towards The Boar's Head.

Althea wanted to run after him, but common sense prevailed. She joined Lizzie in the trap with mixed feelings. She thought about the tear in his shabby coat and wondered about the house that he was so eager to share with her. All that would come to mind was the merest of cottages. She smiled wistfully. He had sounded so proud of it and with all of her heart, she wished that she had been born a village girl and could share his roof.

Lizzie handed the reins to her, a look of disbelief on her face. "What on earth were you thinking of, condescending to the likes of him? He's the reprobate what tried to accost me last year. Nigh frightened me to death, that one did."

Aware that Lizzie had quite forgotten her place, she patted her arm and said, "Your fears were groundless, Lizzie dear. The gentleman mistook you for me."

Lizzie's jaw dropped.

Taking pleasure in confounding Lizzie, she determined not to enlighten her further. Considering the depths of her unhappiness at parting with John Soames, Althea wondered why she had gone out of her way to display such pettiness towards a good friend. Not wishing to delve deeper into what she considered to be her wicked nature, she flicked the reins, and with a clicking noise, galvanized the pony into heading for Camberly Hall.

Without even bothering to change her clothes, Althea went to the library, rang for Jarvis, and asked him to inform the marquis that she would like to see him. The marquis lost no time in joining her.

She was pacing the floor when he entered, and after inquiring after his health, invited him to sit down on a large chair covered in bronze-colored cut velvet, which she knew to be a favorite of his.

The marquis complied, then laced his fingers together and gazed at her expectantly. Althea fought back the temptation to tell him she had decided not to marry Philippe. Only the fear that she would seek out John Soames and agree to marry him prevented her from doing so.

Without any preliminaries, Althea came right to the point. "Uncle, after careful consideration, I have decided to follow your sage advice and marry Philippe—that is, if he is agreeable to the idea."

The marquis beamed. "A beautiful young lady such as you who is also kind and virtuous? Without a doubt, *chérie*, Philippe will consider it both an honor and a pleasure to marry you."

"Of course, Philippe must understand that my father left

the interests of Camberly in the very capable hands of his friend, Lord Shrewsbury."

"Eh? But surely when you marry, that all changes?"

"I am afraid not. It in no way calls Philippe's honor to question, but Papa was merely protecting the future of the earldom against fortune hunters and wastrels."

"But what of Philippe's pride? It is only natural for a lady to lean on her husband for guidance. Surely it can be changed in the courts?"

"I am sorry, Uncle, but even if it were possible I would not agree to it. I could not go against Papa's dying wishes."

Althea watched his face as it ran the gamut of emotion from frustrated fury to outraged dignity, ending in deprecating acquiescence.

"There is one more condition."

"And what might that be?" He sounded defeated.

"The wedding must take place before June has passed. The last Saturday of the month, to be precise."

"But I do not understand. Such haste is most unseemly."

"Uncle, if you wish this marriage to take place, I suggest that you ensure that Philippe procures a license before I have time to change my mind."

The marquis looked hurt. "Really, Althea, your attitude is most disturbing. This is a side of you I have never seen before. How can you be so lacking in heart?"

I have a heart, Uncle, but it is broken into a thousand pieces and does not work as well as it should.

"Forgive me, Uncle. I do not mean to sound unfeeling, but is it not natural for a young lady to feel nervous when contemplating her approaching nuptials?"

Seemingly mollified by her words, he smiled. "Quite so, *chérie*. Now if you will excuse me, I think I shall take my afternoon nap."

With a bow, he departed the room, slamming the door behind him. Althea was left with a sinking feeling that with its closing, all chances for her future happiness were doomed.

Chapter 12

The next morning, in a desperate effort to postpone facing Philippe, Althea confined herself to the east wing of Camberly Hall, looking for signs of mildew. Later, she found it had been unnecessary, because he did not leave his chamber all day, pleading a slight malaise.

However, the next afternoon, as she sat in her sewing room embroidering a rose on a square of cambric, Philippe poked his head around the door, a tentative smile on his face. With a sinking feeling, Althea smiled in return.

"Feeling better, are you?"

"Hmm?"

"I was told that you were indisposed. A slight malaise?"

"Oh, yes. I am feeling a lot better, thank you." As he spoke, his gaze shifted from side to side as if he found it difficult to look her squarely in the eye. "It is good of you to ask."

A deadly silence followed. Althea fought the urge to fidget. *For goodness' sake, Philippe, do get on with it!*

Mercifully, he reopened the conversation. "Althea? We are jolly good friends, do you not agree?"

"I would have to say that we rub along fairly well."

Philippe looked hurt. "That does not sound very warm. What makes you say such a thing?"

Althea wished she had not been so candid but plunged ahead, hoping that honesty would bring them closer together. "Good friends trust one another with their innermost thoughts. You are far too reserved for that."

Philippe winced. "Good heavens, Althea, I should hope so. Such a lack of restraint is frowned upon in polite Society."

"The disapproval of polite Society has no bearing on the

matter, Philippe. I am referring to the sort of intimacy that exists between good friends."

"Althea, such sentiment is ill-considered. I am of the opinion that restraint should be practiced with even greater diligence when dealing with one's friends. Familiarity of that sort can only result in a loss of respect for one another."

Althea gave up. *By all means observe the proprieties, Philippe. Your dear grandpapa drummed such thoughts into your head from the day you uttered your first sentence. What better way is there to control a small boy than discouraging him from forming close bonds with others?*

"There are two sides to a question, and fortunately, Philippe, we are both free to make up our minds about such things. Just let us agree that for the most part, we get along well enough."

Philippe agreed with alacrity. "I quite agree. In fact, I think we get along rather splendidly."

Althea thought his assessment of their friendship was far too rosy, but was not about to refine on the matter. After all, Philippe would not be comfortable with such an affront to his sense of propriety.

"Yes, Philippe, one might say that."

Philippe beamed, evidently satisfied with so much less than true friendship had to offer.

With a feeling of profound pity, she added a little kindness to the mix. "In fact, I cannot recall one cross word ever passing between us."

This was evidently the encouragement he needed to goad him into action, for without more ado he dropped to one knee and took her hand. For a moment, he just looked at her with a blank look on his face, as if he had forgotten what he was going to say, then he said, "Althea."

Althea held her breath, wondering if he would proceed further.

"Althea."

She exhaled.

"Althea, it would give me infinite joy if you would consent to be my wife."

Althea hesitated before giving him an answer. This would be

the only moment given her to change her mind. To her surprise, Philippe's eyes filled with a look of dread. *He must truly care for me. The poor darling is terrified lest I refuse him.* This is all it took.

She placed her other hand on his head. "I shall be honored to marry you, Philippe dear."

He fumbled in his coat and took out a ring. Putting a firm grip on her hand, he slipped it on her finger. It was a heavy ring, the center stone a large, oval sapphire surrounded by diamonds. The setting slipped around to face her palm.

Philippe looked at her, his beautiful hazel eyes filled with regret "I am sorry about that. We can get it made smaller the next time we go to London. It was the ring that Grandfather gave to my grandmother and, in turn, my father gave to my mother. I suppose it has become a tradition. I have nothing else to offer you."

"Nor would I wish for anything else. Your ring is magnificent, fit for a queen."

Althea said this with all honesty. The ring *was* magnificent. She marveled that her uncle had not sold it years ago. Then she realized that his pride would demand that a de Maligny bride should receive nothing less.

Philippe smiled, and gave her a quick peck on the cheek. Surprised, Althea ran her hand down the side of her face. The kiss was so brief she wondered if he had truly kissed her or whether it had been a figment of her imagination. He turned slightly, as if preparing for flight.

"Wait, Philippe. The other matters. Your grandfather discussed them with you?"

Philippe looked blank for a moment. "You mean my not managing Camberly for you? A trifle odd, but perhaps it is for the better. According to my maternal grandfather, when the time comes, taking care of the Bainbridge estate will be challenge enough for me."

"And the wedding date?"

Philippe frowned. "To be quite frank, Althea, I rather hoped you would reconsider that. Dreadfully precipitous, I thought. Smacks awfully close to being scandalous. Tongues are bound to wag."

"I am sorry, Philippe. This wedding will take place on the last Saturday of the month, or not at all."

Philippe frowned. "Very well, but it is deucedly inconvenient. I am expected in Bedfordshire the end of this week. I suppose I could stop at Doctor's Commons for a license on my way back." He snapped his fingers. "I can also spend Friday night at the house in Brighton and go straight to the church from there on that Saturday. That should work out quite well, I should think."

"Yes, it should."

"Excellent Then it is settled."

Philippe made his bow and left the room before Althea could blink. It gave her pause for thought.

I always imagined that a proposal of marriage would be a wondrous thing, full of declarations of lifelong devotion and references to my beauty and virtue. The offer I received from John Soames was scarcely better, but at least he declared his love with ardent kisses, and if I am any judge, searing ardor. Then what does that swift little kiss from Philippe signify? I shall do well to be married in all haste, lest I run all over Camberly searching for John Soames.

Althea was awakened on her wedding morning by the sunlight streaming through her window. She had spent a restless night so with a groan she pulled the counterpane over her head and cuddled into a ball.

She had scarcely made herself comfortable when Lizzie bustled into the room. "Time for your bath, my lady," she caroled.

Althea cringed. No one should be that cheerful first thing in the morning. It was to no avail. Lizzie pulled the bedclothes back.

Althea sat up and glared at her. "Are you quite mad, Lizzie? The sun has scarcely risen."

"Dawn was a good hour ago. We should get started if we are going to make you look your most beautiful."

Althea stared at Lizzie. *Make me look my most beautiful?* Then it came to her. This was the day she had promised to marry Philippe.

The anguish she had suffered the previous evening over her forthcoming nuptials came back to haunt her. Unable to sleep, she had forsaken her bed and had pulled back the curtains and stared out the window. Her gaze invariably strayed beyond the gardens to where the River Camber spilled out into the ocean.

Althea longed to see a lantern wave among the trees, and wondered how she would respond if it did happen. Would she watch until John Soames grew tired of holding it aloft, or would she toss her bonnet over the windmill and make a mad dash straight into his arms?

Suddenly the enormity of her transgression hit home. *Great heavens, Althea Markham. On the very eve of your marriage to Philippe you are mooning over another man. It will not do—Philippe deserves better.*

She had returned to her bed, convinced that she was dishonorable and not worthy to make her vows in front of the altar at St. Martin's. As she meekly submitted to Lizzie's ministrations, she could think of no extenuating circumstances to change the way she felt.

While Lizzie was vigorously toweling her hair dry, a servant from the kitchen carried in a tray of food and a pot of tea. Lizzie removed the domed covers to reveal a breakfast of toast and fruit. "I thought something light would be wise," Lizzie explained.

"Some tea, perhaps, but I could not eat a bite."

"I am not surprised. This wedding business has all been so quick—you've scarcely had time to catch your breath. Lady Althea, I hope you have thought this through."

Althea had not been called by that honorific since she had been made a countess. She remembered when they were little girls how Lizzie would call after her in a piping little voice: "Lady Althea, wait for me, you are running much too fast."

Perhaps I still am.

Out loud she said, "Do not concern yourself, Lizzie. You worry too much."

Lizzie proceeded to brush Althea's hair a little too vigorously for comfort. Through her looking glass, Althea saw her maid's mouth was clamped into a grim line. Althea feared that her slight rebuke had hurt Lizzie's feelings. It was difficult maintaining a balance between servant and friend.

Lizzie did not utter another word until she had finished dressing Althea's hair. Then, apparently success overriding her hurt feelings, with a triumphant flourish she said, "There, I've finished it. How do you like it, my lady?"

"You have magic in your fingers, Lizzie. I look positively regal."

Lizzie beamed, her hurt feelings evidently soothed.

Celeste accompanied Althea on her carriage ride to the church. The marquis had opted to ride his horse, pleading, "Carriages rattle my bones too much these days." It was to be a very private ceremony—no outsiders had been invited, not even the Swanns.

At the onset of the ride, Althea kept her hands tightly clasped in her lap, her gaze resolutely fixed ahead. Celeste gently broke her fingers loose.

"Relax, darling. There is nothing to fear. You are going to the church to be married, not to the guillotine."

"Perhaps not, Mama."

Althea held her breath, hoping her slip of the tongue had passed unnoticed. The shocked look on her mother's face proved otherwise.

She grasped Althea's arm. "Something is seriously amiss, and I insist on knowing what it is."

Althea could not prevent her lower lip from quivering.

Celeste looked grim. "We are not going a step further until I get to the bottom of this." She called out to the driver, "Stop the carriage, if you please."

The man complied. The marquis caught up with them and leaned over, a questioning look on his face. Celeste waved him on. "It is nothing, Uncle dear. Just a little matter Althea and I neglected to discuss before we left home. Kindly proceed."

Celeste turned to Althea. "Get out of the carriage and start walking. We have to speak in private."

Althea felt very conspicuous walking along the road wearing a wedding veil adorned with the elaborate coronet of white silk roses Lizzie had fashioned for her. It was a relief when her mother said, "You may stop now. I should imagine this is far enough."

She stroked Althea's cheek. "Am I wrong in thinking that you are having second thoughts about this marriage?"

"Mama, I have done a dreadful thing."

The words poured out like a torrent.

Celeste loosened Althea's hold. "Slow down, child. You mean to tell me that our uncle is behind this marriage?"

"At first."

Celeste clenched her fists. "That villain, I could choke him. But wait—I hardly think you would do anything at his behest." She gave Althea a penetrating look. "I am right about that, am I not?"

Althea looked away.

"It is clear that you are not in love with Philippe, so why in heaven's name are you marrying him?"

Althea covered her face with her hands. "Oh dear, I feel so wretched."

Celeste pulled Althea's hands down from her face and held them in a firm grip. "Tell me, Althea. Tell me, my little cabbage—you have carried this burden long enough."

Althea sighed. "Very well, Mama. In any case, I am tired of the whole matter. I agreed to marry Philippe because I was afraid I would weaken and marry someone absolutely beyond the pale."

"And who might that be, *chérie?*"

"Your accomplice, John Soames."

Celeste's eyes widened. "Really? You are in love with John?"

Althea nodded. "One can only assume that I have taken leave of my senses."

"Because you love a fine young man like John Soames?" she said gently. "I cannot agree."

"For goodness' sake, Mama, look what he does. Besides that, he may not love me at all. It could very well be my fortune that interests him."

"There you wrong him, Althea. You have him confused

with the sort of person one meets in our circle. He is far too idealistic to marry where his heart does not lie."

"How can you be sure?"

"I just know. The things he has done for me, even to the point of risking his life. Not once would he accept a penny for his trouble."

"But surely you are not suggesting that I marry him?"

"Of course not. That would have to be your decision. In any case, right now you have enough to think about. Do you really want to go through with this farce of a marriage with our cousin?"

"I am in a quandary. I thought that perhaps I would tell him the truth and let him decide what to do. After all, I want to hurt him as little as possible."

Celeste rolled her eyes. "You know, my darling, I never thought I would be saying such a thing to you, but I fear you have an exaggerated sense of your own importance."

Althea was confused. "I do not understand."

"I mean that if you do not marry Philippe he will get over it. He will not die of grief. You worry about John Soames wishing to marry you for your fortune. Perhaps you should be more concerned about Philippe marrying you because his grandfather wants him to."

"I should hate to believe that of Philippe."

"Open your eyes, Althea. He shows you no affection whatsoever. I had put his odd behavior down to shyness, but good heavens, I have yet to see him hold your hand, or give you so much as a friendly pat, much less steal a kiss."

"He kissed me when I accepted his proposal."

"Tell me, Althea, was it a pleasant experience?"

"Pleasant? It was the same as any other time he has kissed me."

Celeste looked bemused. "Those cousinly pecks on the cheek? Come now, darling, he had you alone. You said you would marry him. Were you not in the least surprised that he did not seize the chance to kiss you on the lips?"

"Mama, looking back, I cannot believe how dense I was. I

convinced myself that only the lower orders allowed free rein to their passions."

"You mean men like John Soames? Oh dear, I *have* neglected your education. Darling, if *that* were the case, our sort would have died out long ago."

"In retrospect I suppose it *does* sound foolish. I just so desperately wanted everything to be right."

Celeste responded with a giggle. "John Soames's kisses must have been exceptionally agreeable to have inspired that mad dash for the altar with the first gentleman you could find."

Althea thought about those kisses and smiled. "Yes, Mama, they were *wonderful.*"

"Then it is agreed?"

"Hmmm?"

"Philippe has to be told that the marriage will not take place."

Celeste signaled to the driver to bring the carriage forward, and they proceeded to St. Martin's.

When they arrived at the church, they were surprised to see another carriage waiting outside in the care of an attendant wearing the green-and-gold livery of Philippe's other grandfather, Baron Bainbridge.

Althea groaned. "Oh, dear. I had not counted on his grandparents being here. This is going to prove most difficult."

Celeste squeezed her hand. "Stand your ground, darling. Remember, this is as much for Philippe's sake as your own."

As they entered the church vestibule, the baron came forward to greet them, the marquis following closely behind.

Althea managed a weak smile. "Lord Bainbridge. What a pleasant surprise."

The baron looked sober. "I wish that were so. You see, Althea dear, it is my misfortune to be the bearer of bad news."

Althea clutched her throat. "Philippe has been hurt."

The baron shook his head. "I almost wish that were the case. It would be the only honorable reason for him not being here."

He turned to the marquis. "Most of the responsibility for this debacle, sir, lies squarely at your door."

On thus being attacked, the marquis seemed to sag, reminding Althea of a ragdoll that had lost some of its stuffing.

The baron turned his attention to Althea once more. "You see, two days ago Philippe eloped with a Miss Nancy Milford, the daughter of a friend of mine. He had every intention of honoring his promise to marry you on his arrival at Bainbridge, but according to the letter he left in his chamber, Miss Milford informed him that she was carrying his child."

"How ironic," Althea murmured, and to her own consternation began to laugh. She looked to her mother and shook her head, making a gesture that clearly stated she was helpless to do otherwise.

Celeste drew Althea into an embrace. "Ah *chérie*, this is one of life's more delicious ironies. If nothing else, I should hope that this has taught you to leave the big problems in the lap of God." Having said that, she, too, broke into laughter.

Philippe's grandfathers exchanged baffled looks. Then the baron cleared his throat and with a look of deep concern, said, "I say, de Maligny, I would advise you to get your kinswomen home as quickly as possible and then summon a doctor. I fear this shocking affair has completely unhinged them."

Chapter 13

John ran his hands over the books in the library, delighting in the texture of their rich leather bindings. Of all the rooms in the house he had inherited from his Aunt Gertrude, the library and its contents was his favorite.

He moved over to a huge, diamond-paned window and looked outside where a garden descended to a sandy beach in a series of terraces.

"Our own hanging gardens," his aunt used to say. "I doubt Babylon's were any more beautiful."

Recalling her words filled John with a bittersweet sadness. "I hope they had a garden equally as lovely waiting for you in paradise, sweet lady," he murmured.

Beyond the gardens, Camberly Bay made a sweeping arc to the left of the house. Several fishing boats dotted the harbor and in front of one of the cottages on the shore a fisherman was mending his net.

John recalled the misery he had endured while occupying the neighboring cottage and shuddered. "Nothing you can say or do would induce me to repeat that nightmare, brother dear."

"What nightmare might that be, old chap?"

John started at the sound of Marcus's voice.

Marcus looked askance. "Try and pull yourself together. If you go around talking to yourself, people will think you have gone round the bend."

John smiled, feeling a little sheepish at being caught at a disadvantage in front of his oh-so-suave older sibling.

"Where did you spring from? Reeves must be falling down on the job, leaving guests to wander about like that."

"Do not blame Reeves. I told him I would announce myself.

And besides, I am family, not company."

Marcus joined him at the window. "I say, I do envy you your view. I have always admired the way all those towers and turrets of Camberly Hall rise above those trees across the bay."

"That is the only part of the panorama that I would just as lief not be able to see."

John regretted the outburst almost immediately. Marcus subjected him to a searching look. "I say, John. Cannot imagine why I did not see it right off the bat, but you look positively hagridden. Something happen that I should know about?"

"No. I was just reminiscing over some of the things that Aunt Gertrude used to say and do, and it saddened me."

"You are bound to feel that way for a while. This place is full of memories. But that isn't the reason for your dreadful appearance and you know it. I would say you have been spending a lot of time drowning your sorrows in spirits of some sort and it has to do with Camberly Hall—or more to the point, someone who lives there. The dowager is not your type, so it has to be her daughter. You are suffering from unrequited love for Althea Markham."

"Try not to be so ridiculous. There is nothing between Althea Markham and me. She was married last Saturday, if you must know."

"Must I?" Marcus replied, an arch expression on his face. "And how did you come to know of this?"

"Er—Reeves happened to mention it, I believe. It is hard to keep that sort of thing quiet in a village as small as Camberly." John dropped his gaze to his shoes, shamefaced for having told a deliberate lie.

Marcus laid his hand on John's shoulder. "You had to have obtained that piece of intelligence directly from Althea. Truth be told, she did *not* get married last Saturday."

John shrugged free of Marcus's hand. "She lied to me? I tell you, Marcus, the females of the species are more treacherous than snakes."

"No more so than the males, I would venture. You see, poor Althea was left in the lurch at the altar."

John was overcome by a wash of pity and outrage over Althea's plight. "I say, what dastard did that? The bounder should be horsewhipped."

"*Dastard* is a strong word. The groom was her cousin, Philippe de Maligny, a mere minnow up against his barracuda of a grandfather, I fear. He told the marquis that he was in love with the daughter of one of his other grandfather's neighbors in Bedfordshire—a young lady by the name of Nancy Milford— well dowered and everything, but the old pirate would have none of it."

"What possible reason could that dreadful old man have for destroying his grandson's chance for happiness?"

"One does not have to be a genius to come up with an answer. Before the revolution, the marquis was rich, powerful—a man of great consequence." Marcus punctuated each point with a gesture. "Even in his present circumstances, his arrogance defies description. Philippe is in line for a barony, but that does not satisfy the marquis. I believe he would sacrifice his own mother if it would afford him a British earldom for his issue. Need more be said?"

"How are you privy to such knowledge?"

"I happened to call at Camberly Hall that very afternoon and Celeste confided in me."

"And right away you told me?"

"Naturally, I presume it will go no further."

"I should hope not. You know, Father always drummed into us that three may only keep a secret if two of them happen to be dead."

"Now you are being tiresome. As I see it, you were the only person outside of her family who knew about Althea's wedding. One can only conclude that you were let in on the secret as a means of softening the blow when your suit was rejected."

John shrugged Marcus's hand away from his shoulder. "Kindly refrain from jumping to conclusions, Marcus. It is extremely irritating."

"Oh, stop it, John. Your feeble attempt to gammon me is beyond all reason, but I shall overlook it because you are obviously distressed and you are my brother. I would hope that you could confide in me at such a time."

Marcus gestured toward an armchair facing the hearth. "Sit down. I shall pour us some brandy and then you may tell me what happened."

Marcus's voice was soothing. John capitulated and sat down as he had suggested. "You will find some very fine cognac over on the table. One of the few advantages of being a smuggler of sorts. I am more than ready for a glass or two."

Marcus poured the amber liquid into two large crystal goblets and joined John by the hearth. He handed one of them to him. "Here. A little cognac will benefit both of us, I should imagine."

He sat on a matching chair on the other side of the hearth, then raised his glass. "To health and happiness, John."

John responded with a hollow laugh.

"Oh, dear. Is it as bad as all that?"

"Where would you like to me to begin?"

"I shall presume that you fell in love with Althea one night by the river on the wrong side of midnight I shall also presume that perhaps a few kisses were exchanged for you to dare to think that she would look favorably on your offer. So why not get to the part where you actually got down on your knees and asked for her hand?"

"I did not do that—get on my knees, that is, and I asked her twice. The first time *was* by the river, and we did kiss. Marcus, I will not go into the details—it would not be the thing. Just let me say that the very first time we kissed, something ignited between us. I know she felt it, too. We are so right for each other—there is no other way of putting it."

"And the second time?"

"That was on the esplanade, just before I met you at The Boar's Head last. I cannot for the life of me fathom why I allowed things to get so out of hand. After Belinda's perfidy I vowed I would never give another woman the opportunity to inflict that sort of damage again."

He drank deeply of the cognac. "I do not understand,

Marcus. I know Althea loves me and I told her I was well able to take care of her. Even suggested that she come live with me under my roof, but it would not do. Tell me, brother, does not anyone marry for love these days?"

Marcus smiled. "Love makes a paperscull of the best of men. It was John Soames whom Althea rejected, not John Ridley, and rightly so. As I recall you came to The Boar's Head that afternoon looking little better than a ragpicker. Really, John, even smugglers have their standards. The poor girl probably thought you were bent on housing her in a fisherman's cottage."

"Where do I go from here? I doubt that Althea is receptive to anyone's suit after being treated so shamefully. Besides, I shudder to think how she would react if she finds out I have been deceiving her all these months."

"First of all, you *have* to tell her. Play up the fact that it was government policy to keep your identity secret."

"Then?"

"Really, John, I thought it was perfectly simple. You tell her—in your own words, of course—that you realize your courtship was a trifle precipitous and you would like to start all over. You know, get to know her better—that sort of thing."

John groaned. "God. I think I would far rather face a cage full of lions."

Marcus grinned. "So would I, old chap. At no time did I say it would be easy."

Althea was sitting in her sewing room, diligently plying her needle to her embroidery. She had not made much progress with the work, having just put the final stitch to the very first rose when her mother entered and said, "There is a gentleman to see you."

"Oh? And whom might that be?"

"I think he had better tell you himself."

Althea felt her scalp prickle. "Mama, what sort of mischief are you up to now?"

"*La,* child. You wound me. All I ask is that you hear what he has to say and give it your kind consideration. But then, I know you will do that, bless your sweet nature."

Althea found these honeyed words downright unsettling. Of one thing she was certain—her mother could not possibly be up to anything good and there was only one way to find out what it was.

"Very well, Mama, show the gentleman in."

Celeste left the room and John entered in her stead. At first, Althea did not recognize the impeccably dressed young man. She was too dazzled by the shine of his top boots and the cut of his fawn-colored coat to take in his features. When her gaze finally locked with his, she rose to her feet, her mouth agape.

"Mr. Soames?"

He bowed. "That is a matter I have to clear up."

"Yes, I rather think you do, but first, may I offer you some refreshment?"

"Thank you, no. I have recently partaken of an adequate breakfast"

"Then pray be seated," she said, and sank back into her chair.

All the time Althea was trying to observe the amenities of polite society, she was trying to make sense of the transformation that had taken place in John Soames's appearance and manner.

His clothes not only bespoke the rank of a gentleman, they were of a quality that proclaimed his position among the very cream of the *ton*.

She supposed smuggling *could* be that profitable, but seriously doubted it. Then it occurred to her that at one time or another he had discarded the soft cadence of the local yoemanry in favor of the well-modulated tones of a gentleman. John Soames had grievously deceived her.

A feeling of righteous indignation welled up in her. "It would appear that you have made me the victim of some cruel hoax, sir."

"On my honor, Althea, I swear to you that was not my intention. When I embarked on this course of smuggling and intrigue, you were a stranger to me, a name heard mentioned only in passing. Then when I met your mother, I learned more about you."

"There, I fear, you have the advantage of me, Mr. Soames."

"That is a point I should clear up right away. My name is Ridley, John Ridley. Marcus is my brother."

"I see. I am very disappointed to learn that Lord Ridley would indulge in such childish games."

"I am sorry you see our endeavors to help our country in that light, my dear. Although I must admit to harboring doubts from time to time as to the value of the services I perform."

John leaned forward. "Do you not see? It was necessary that I use another name. Marcus thought it might sway you to my side if I said it was at the insistence of those in government, but that was not the case."

"I must admit, Mr. Soames—er, Ridley, I do not see at all. To me, the whole matter is completely mystifying."

"On the contrary, Althea, I changed my name for the same reason your mother went into France disguised as a peasant—we both sought to protect our respective families. If one is caught, the enemy may well seek reprisals against one's relations."

Althea found his words disturbing in the extreme. On what sort of merry chase had he led Mama, with his talk of capture and retribution against loved ones?

"Mr. Ridley, I find it absolutely reprehensible that you encouraged my mother to take such risks."

"Encouraged your mother? Althea, both Marcus and I spent *hours* trying to talk her out of it. Do you think I relished the extra danger involved in taking a gentlewoman with me to France?"

"You could have refused."

"I did, at first. But she was determined to make the trip with or without me." He shrugged. "What would you have had me do? Stand by and watch while she hired the scum of the docks, who most assuredly would have murdered her for her gold and cast her body into the sea?"

"I am indebted to you for taking care of my mother, Mr. Ridley. I know only too well that once she takes the bit between her teeth, she is unstoppable."

"Not at all, and please, Althea, call me John. Do not push me away with all that formality."

"That is something I prefer to consider at a future date. That privilege was accorded to a Mr. Soames, a gentleman who now appears never to have existed. You, Mr. Ridley, I know not at all."

"Ah, but you do. I am the one you kissed by the river. Remember? The moon turned the river to silver, and those kisses turned the blood in our veins to fire."

Althea felt her cheeks turn pink. Such intemperate words for an English gentleman to be uttering! And oh, how delicious they sounded!

Looking as cold and as disapproving as she knew how, she rebuked him. "Mr. Ridley. Please comport yourself as becomes a gentleman, or I shall be prevailed upon to ask you to leave."

To her dismay, he did not seem one whit concerned; to the contrary, his expression seemed to be one of high amusement. "I must say, Althea, you do that awfully well."

"Do what, pray?" she replied frostily.

"Play the high-in-the-instep *grande dame*. Give yourself a few years, and you will be the most formidable lady of the *ton.*"

"I must say, for someone who wishes to get in my good graces you have a very peculiar way of going about it."

"Not at all. You complained of not knowing me. If I tiptoe around you, kissing the hem of your dress every time I say or do something that makes you blush from the top of your pretty head right down to your toes, you will never get to know me, will you? And I, in turn, shall be denied the pleasure of hearing you call me by my first name with your oh-so-very-seductive voice."

Althea laughed in spite of herself. "Sir, I suspect that even you do not believe half of what you say."

He leaned forward and gazed intently at her with his clear, gray eyes. *"Brava,* Althea, that is much better. Without a little lightheartedness to our natures, life would stretch before us one joyless day after another."

His words struck a chord. "That is something my mother might have said. Indeed, I do believe she did. Worded a little differently, perhaps, but the meaning was the same."

"Without such an outlook on life, I doubt your mother would have come through the horrors she experienced in her youth half so well. She winnowed away the ugliness and sorrow and made her bread out of all that is good in life."

Althea thought this over, wondering why this man who had known her mother but briefly had recognized her strength in the face of adversity, whereas she had only seen frivolity. Suddenly, Althea felt very small.

"I love my mother very much, but until you pointed it out, I did not see her qualities in such heroic terms. I am led to believe that you have a very generous spirit."

John made a deprecating gesture. "One does not have to be clairvoyant to see that in your mother's case, happiness was a deliberate choice."

As in yours? Althea pondered. She studied him closely. He was pleasant-looking enough, but most likely she was the only female whose heart beat faster when he smiled. Of a certainty, he did not possess the sort of devastating manly beauty that caused foolish young girls to swoon. On top of that, he no doubt had had to come to terms with being a second son. In other words, all his life he had had to contend with being Marcus Ridley's younger brother.

"Happiness a deliberate choice? That is a lovely thought to which I shall give more consideration."

"As shall I."

She raised a brow. "Do you mean to tell me that you do not practice what you preach?"

"By and large, but some sorrows in life are very hard to surmount. For instance, when the love of one's life refuses to marry one."

"And who might that be, sir?"

"I am not sure. You see, John Soames fell in love with a little governess who put him in his place, then stormed out of his life. By George, that slip of a girl carried it off with all the hauteur of a grand duchess."

"Mr. Soames fell in love with a figment of his imagination."

"Perhaps. But John Ridley is in love with a tender, passionate young lady who is very real. Given time, there is a possibility she might return his love."

The humor left his face to be replaced by a desperate earnestness. "All I ask, Althea, is for permission to pay you court. Let us get to know one another and find out what is real and what is not."

Althea rose to end the interview. With a look of devastation, he followed suit Althea was touched. His distress looked very real.

She held out her hand—something she rarely did, and certainly not without others present. "I shall look forward to your next visit—John."

He broke into a smile, the expression on his face reminding Althea of the way the sun sometimes pierces the clouds after a sudden summer storm.

"Let it be tomorrow, Althea. We could ride into Camberly and take a walk on the pier, perhaps stop for refreshments at that little tearoom on the esplanade."

"And have tongues wagging from here to Brighton?"

He shook his head. "Althea, you surprise me. With your regal presence, I did not picture you as the sort of young lady who gave a fig for what other people think."

She looked arch. "I believe you have me confused with the older Lady Camberly."

"Then you refuse?"

"Of course not—I was merely pointing out the consequences of such behavior."

He bent down and kissed the tip of her nose.

"You know, Althea, I believe you are more like your mother than you realize. You are only just coming into your own."

"My mother is a very formidable lady. The average gentleman would flee from here as fast as his horse could carry him."

He grinned. "We Ridleys are made of sterner stuff. I shall be on your doorstep promptly at three o'clock tomorrow afternoon."

Althea watched his horse carry him the length of the approach to the house. It wasn't until he was out of sight that she realized there was a huge smile pasted on her face.

Chapter 14

John arrived at the portals to Camberly Hall, driving a black curricle pulled by a pair of perfectly matched grays. The horses had been groomed until their coats had taken on the sheen of polished marble.

Before the carriage came to a complete stop, his tiger, Grimes, leaped from his perch in the back ready to settle them. A groom brought from the stables in expectation of John's arrival came to Grimes's aid, and each held a horse firmly under control.

John had climbed only the first three of seven steps when Althea came through the great double doors. The sight of her took his breath away.

She was clad in a curricle coat in a kerseymere of pale sea green. A dress whose color reminded John of a robin's egg made a subtle contrast. This ensemble was matched with a silk bonnet of the same sea green, with matching ribbons securing it under her chin. The underside of the brim was fashioned out of a ruched silk, matching the color of her dress.

She waited for him on the top step. "*La*, sir," she called out. "What a handsome pair of grays. They go so well with your carriage."

John warmed to her praise, then felt somewhat sheepish that her approval meant so much to him. Especially since it was not completely deserved.

"Thank you," he replied, and then bowed to her. "I inherited the grays from my aunt. Fine horseflesh was one of my Uncle John's few extravagances. The curricle is one of mine."

He offered her his arm and led her down the steps. He then handed her into the carriage, a gallantry that required very little effort on his part, for she proved to be extremely nimble. When she was comfortably settled, he climbed next to her on the driver's seat.

Once he had the spirited horses well in hand, the groom and the tiger got out of the way, the latter jumping back into position at the rear of the carriage.

John could not believe his good fortune. What could be more blissful than to drive his curricle under the sun-dappled trees of the Camberly Hall approach with Althea Markham by his side?

He was acutely aware of a thrill of excitement passing between them. She smiled at him. His throat convulsed and his heart began to pound. He found he could scarcely breathe, much less hold a conversation.

As they approached the outskirts of Camberly, he leaned toward her, intending to break the silence with an inane remark regarding the weather, at the same time she did.

He was so enthralled by the elfin quality of her pale green eyes, he quite forgot what he was going to say.

Althea was the first to look away, seemingly interested in her gloved hands which were demurely folded in her lap. He saw her face and throat slowly diffuse into a rosy glow.

She feels as I do. Oh, Lord, I hope this does not turn out to be one of those elaborate mating dances. I cannot endure much more of this.

They drove past the pier and Althea thought fondly of their first meeting. The man she knew as John Soames had been able to look beyond her dowdy appearance and consider her beautiful. She had spurned George Delville's offer of marriage for the opposite reason.

Could it be that John Ridley is in love with me? I pray so. I cannot endure the thought of it being otherwise.

She chided herself for allowing her unfortunate experience with Nigel Fortescue to give her cause to doubt John's sincerity. After all, did not Mama vouchsafe his character?

Keeping this in mind, she set aside her worries and scanned the esplanade to see if anyone she knew was taking the air, but to no avail. It seemed that Camberly attracted more strangers all the time. Then in the distance she saw two men who seemed familiar to her come out of The Boar's Head and walk in their direction. One was tall and thin, his companion shorter and rather stout.

When they drew nearer, she recognized them and tugged on John's sleeve. "Those two men."

"Which ones? There are quite a few gentlemen squiring their ladies along the esplanade."

"I doubt you would call them gentlemen. Look. They are about to walk past Hansford's."

"Hmm. I see what you mean. How on earth did you come to know such a seedy-looking pair?"

"They came to the Hall to visit my uncle."

"Did they indeed? I do not mean to be rude, but one cannot help wonder what dealings he could possibly have with such as they. French, I take it?"

Althea nodded. "Monsieur Joubert is the taller one. His friend's name eludes me for the moment." She leaned forward. "Why, they just entered Hansford's."

"You find that odd?"

"Every bit as much as my uncle's gracious condescension toward them."

John shrugged. "They could be buying dress stuffs for their wives. People from all over patronize the place. But of course I do not have to tell you that."

"On a Sunday? It is rumored that Mr. Hansford has smugglers to thank for the variety of his goods. Perhaps that is the answer. It would certainly explain where my uncle gets his cognac." She looked at him and smiled. "For a while, I *thought* he was getting it from you."

His eyes widened. "Did you, now? I am afraid you are wrong about that. Mind you, I would not be at all surprised if they turned out to be smugglers, but they are not likely to ply their nefarious trade in broad daylight, are they?" He shook his head. "No. I would have to say that they must have another reason for calling on our friend Hansford."

"Then you agree that they *could* be smugglers?"

"Absolutely. They could be anything. Anything except exiled emigres, that is. Nothing in their bearing suggests to me that they might be aristocrats."

His words gave Althea a sense of unease. When John reined the horses at the teashop, the pastries it was noted for had lost their appeal for Althea, so she begged off the treat. He claimed not to mind.

"In any case," he said, "it looks deucedly crowded in there."

They came to the pier once more, and John asked her if she would care to take a stroll. "Rekindle the memory of our first meeting?"

In view of the people already crowding the pier, Althea was tempted to refuse him. From the start, his anxiety had hovered over them like a thick fog. She decided that a little lighthearted teasing might clear the air.

She put her index finger to her cheek and pretended to consider the matter. "You wish to rekindle the memory of our first trip? That poses a problem."

"How?"

"With whom shall I take this memorable walk? The respectable Mr. Ridley or the outrageous Mr. Soames?"

"Mr. Ridley?"

Althea gave him what she hoped was a saucy smile. "Pity. You see, it will not be the same without Mr. Soames."

By this time they were on the pier and John did not pick up the gauntlet she had tossed him until they had walked several yards.

"So Mr. Soames's company is preferable to mine? That is most distressing."

"Oh, I find you quite amiable, Mr. Ridley, but he is the one whom I met here."

John sighed. "Soames lays claim to the pier *and* the riverbank so I must need to create my own memories with you—but what is left?"

She pretended to ponder the question. "It is hard to say. The tail of the north wind? Or the rainbow's end, perhaps?"

He cast her a sly look. "Or, I could steal Soames's boat—

which is not really his, incidentally—poor chap has not a farthing to his name—and we can claim the seven seas for our very own."

Althea gave his arm a tap. "Fie, Mr. Ridley. And to think that I took Mr. Soames for the greater rascal."

"So you think that I am a rascal?"

"Without a doubt,"

He inclined his head and whispered in her ear. "I am very happy to hear it."

"And why would that be?"

"Because, my dear Lady Camberly, I have a strong suspicion that you have a soft place in your heart for rascals."

Althea pretended to be shocked. "You, sir, are beyond redemption."

As she anticipated, her rebuke was countered with a wicked grin. The tension had been replaced with jollity. The rest of the afternoon could prove to be pleasant.

Being more relaxed allowed them to enjoy their surroundings. John pointed out the amusing antics of the seagulls as they wheeled overhead, waiting to scavenge what they could from the nearby fishing boats.

Althea laughed out loud when one rapacious bird stole a scrap of offal from the beak of another while they were both in full flight.

Only then did she realize that they had become the objects of the questioning stares of ill-mannered bystanders. The final indignity was delivered when the gossipmongers huddled closer together to add their own opinions anent the scandal concerning the local countess which was obviously brewing under their noses.

As far as Althea was concerned, the pier had lost its appeal. As the person around whom everyone and everything in Camberly revolved, she regretted having exposed herself to the idle speculations of those who had nothing better to do with their time.

She looked imploringly at John. "If you please, I should like to go home now. I hate being stared at."

John looked wry. "So I notice. But surely you are used to that? It happens to our family quite frequently. It is best to ignore them."

"I know you are right but lately I have been forced to endure far too much of that sort of thing."

He was instantly contrite. "Forgive my thoughtlessness—we shall leave immediately."

Chapter 15

John called on Althea the following morning to inquire after her health. The incident with the gossips on the pier had been a revelation to him. It was clear that years of humiliation at the hands of opportunists had taken their toll.

As he waited for the door to be opened, he clenched his fists in outrage, wishing he could beat senseless every knave who had caused his beloved even a moment's anguish.

Jarvis invited him in, but shook his head upon hearing that he wished to see the mistress of Camberly.

"I regret to inform you, sir, that her ladyship is not receiving visitors today."

"Then her headache is no better?"

Jarvis fixed his eyes somewhat to the left of John's head. "I cannot say, sir. I was not informed."

John thanked him and turned to leave, his thoughts in turmoil.

She is slipping away from me. The poor girl is afraid to entrust her heart to any man.

He was about to exit the door Jarvis held open for him when a feminine voice, which he recognized as Celeste Markham's melodious contralto, called out to him.

"If you are looking for Althea, try the lily pond. That is where she can usually be found at this hour."

"Not this time, Lady Camberly. Jarvis just told me she is not at home to anyone right now. I rather suspect that she has yet to recover from the headache she incurred yesterday."

Celeste looked thoughtful. "Do you think so? I suppose that would account for her not coming down to breakfast this morning. In any case, I am hurt that you did not see fit to pay me a little visit."

He bowed to her. "My abject apologies, Lady Camberly."

"Unless you stop that Lady Camberly nonsense this instant, your apologies will go unheeded."

She linked her arm through his. "Come now, let me walk you to your carriage. I have been told by one of the grooms that you have the handsomest of curricles. Your horses I have seen many a time, of course. You have no idea how much I envied your late uncle his magnificent grays, and now you, of course."

They had reached the carriage and she patted the flank of the horse closest to her. "There is no help for it. From this day forth you are the recipient of my never-ending envy."

John suspected that Althea's mother was striving a little too hard to be amiable.

He forced a smile. "It is whispered in some circles that the dowager of Camberly Hall handles the racing ribbons as well as any man."

She laughed outright. "That must be one of the mildest things that is said of me in most circles."

"Most of it undeserved. One day, I hope to tell all of those gossips how they have maligned you."

She looked horrified. "Pray reconsider. I should hate everyone to find out how dull my life *really* is."

He saw how wistful she looked and realized there was a kernel of truth behind the banter. Celeste Markham had probably missed a lot of life's sweeter moments.

"I presume you will attend the Prince Regent's grand midsummer fete on the nineteenth?"

"I expect so. I have heard it will be a dreadful crush."

"You have heard aright. Marcus says it will be on a scale unheard-of since the days of the Caesars."

"In that case, how can one refuse? It will most likely be talked about for generations to come."

"And while we are in Town, nothing would give me greater pleasure than to see you handle the ribbons to my curricle."

Her face lit up. "That is excessively kind of you. I think I should enjoy that far more than Prinny's gaudy affair."

As soon as John departed, the smile left her face and she went inside with the determination of one bent on a mission.

Althea, who was in her sewing room diligently embroidering yet a third rose on her square of cambric, had heard everything. When her mother reentered the house, Althea detected anger in the sound of her footsteps.

They stopped directly at her door, and her mother walked in without even bothering to knock, the curve of her generously proportioned mouth pressed into a straight line. Althea decided to meet her head-on.

"Thank you for telling John that I was not at breakfast."

Celeste did not respond right away, and when she pulled up a flimsy little chair and sat down next to her, as closely as possible, Althea knew she was in for a difficult time.

"The falsehood was for his benefit, not yours. I take it that on closer acquaintance you have decided that Mr. Ridley does not measure up to your high standards?"

Althea lowered her eyes. "Something of the sort."

"Daughter, I did not take you for a coward. How could you hide behind the coattails of your butler in such a craven fashion?" Celeste's tone expressed profound disappointment. "Tell me, do you intend to apprise him of your disinterest in his courtship, or will you continue to keep him knocking at your door until he decides that for himself?"

"Of course I shall speak to him. What do you take me for? But not today. I have to choose my words carefully so as to do the least amount of harm."

Celeste stroked Althea's cheek. "La, child. I am thinking that however kindly your rejection is worded, it will not lessen the hurt. I happen to think that John is terribly in love with you."

Althea jerked her head away. "You cannot know that. My experiences make it hard for me to trust any man. When all those dreadful people on the pier started to talk about me, every hurt and humiliation I ever suffered at the hands of rich mushrooms and impoverished lords rushed back to hurt me anew."

"And you are punishing a fine young man who truly loves you because of these creatures?"

"You cannot possibly know how he feels about me. I want to believe him but I am afraid. I love him so much that if he proved untrue, I swear to you, Mama, I would shrivel up and die."

Celeste took Althea's hand and held it to her own cheek. "Neither life nor love comes with guarantees. Be careful, my darling, lest you throw away the latter, for it will color everything else that you do in this life."

Althea's entourage arrived at the house in Mayfair on the sixteenth of June in plenty of time to prepare for the Prince Regent's grand midsummer fete. Rumor had it that two thousand people would attend.

Althea was not enthusiastic about going, even though they were to be among those invited to sit at the prince's table in the Gothic conservatory. Since sending John away, her life had dragged by, one gray day after another.

His absence left her feeling a terrible sense of loss. She found that tears came easily and were difficult to hide from both family and servants.

During one such teary episode her mother came upon her in the library.

"There, there, my little cabbage, tell Mama what is troubling you," she crooned.

Althea turned aside. "It is nothing. I just wish that we had not received the invitation to the Regent's tiresome affair, that is all. You know how much I despise being in the City."

"Poor darling. Nothing you do these days seems to be worth the effort, does it?"

"*Exactly.* Mama, does it not also strike you that way?"

"No, it does not."

Althea wrung her hands together. "Then what is the matter with me? Life seems so—"

"Pointless?"

"I was going to say gray, but pointless will serve. Am I ill, do you suppose?"

"Ah. Did I not warn you that if you deny love, nothing else in life much matters? Go to John and tell him that you love him."

"I would not know where to find him. He left Camberly the very same day I sent him away. He did not tell his household staff where he was going or when he was coming back."

"Who told you that?"

"Jarvis, of course."

Celeste was triumphant. "I have it on good authority that John will be attending this evening's festivities."

"Jarvis, again?"

"But of course. Servants know about our comings and goings almost before we do. Perhaps you will be able to put things right with John tonight."

Althea was torn. "I am not sure. Suppose I marry him and then find out that he does not love me? I would be absolutely devastated."

"And at this moment you are dancing for joy?"

"Do not tease, Mama."

"Let me put it another way. Suppose you marry him and discover that you are the moon and stars to him? Is it not worth the chance to trade a misery you *know* you are suffering for the possibility of achieving a lifetime of bliss?"

Mama makes a lot of sense. But then, she has a gift for getting to the heart of things. She faces life with courage and fortitude, and as her daughter, I should do no less.

"Are you suggesting that I accost him this evening?"

"Not exactly. I have arranged through Marcus for John to come to you. Now, all that is needed is for you to agree."

Althea gave her a heartfelt hug. "Thank you, Mama—that would be much better."

The rest of the morning, Althea's voice was heard all over the house, singing songs about country maidens and their lovers.

Promptly at nine that evening, Althea and her mother and uncle joined other notables in a large reception room to await the arrival of their host. Marcus Ridley took his place beside Althea.

All the ladies were dazzlingly arrayed in their finest evening dresses. Althea looked beautiful in the green-and-lavender shot

silk. It was fashioned in a grand manner, complete with a train and a heart-shaped bodice embroidered with tiny opals.

Celeste's dress was a flattering shade of peach, overlaid with a copper-colored mesh. It was the perfect foil for her fiery hair. Marcus complimented both ladies on their choices.

The gentlemen were elegantly attired in full court dress. Marcus wore a coat of rich dark blue teamed with black breeches and hose. Althea deemed his black leather slippers to be particularly elegant.

The prince was to be joined by exiled members of the French royal family; the room had been hung in blue silk wall hangings with fleur-de-lis richly embroidered with gold thread.

Althea overheard one querulous gentleman say, "As if our battling prince has not spent enough on this affair."

Althea was shocked. "I wonder how one gentleman can disparage another while partaking of his hospitality?" she whispered to Marcus.

Marcus bent his head low to reply. "He is not a gentleman, my dear, not in the truest sense of the word. He happens to be a poet."

"Really?" Althea gave him a closer look. "Lord Byron looks more the part, I fear."

Marcus laughed out loud, and received a chastising glare from the poet for his trouble.

The prince entered the room at a quarter after nine. He was resplendent in the uniform of a field marshal, a rank he had had the foresight to bestow upon himself directly after assuming the title of Prince Regent.

The exiled members of the French royal family were then ushered in, their high-bridged Bourbon noses making them easy to recognize. After a lengthy exchange of tributes, larded with flowery compliments between host and guests, dinner was announced.

Marcus escorted Althea into the Gothic conservatory. The room was a good two hundred feet in length and the table was not much shorter. They were placed about halfway down, a comfortable distance from the coterie of royalty surrounding the prince at the head.

Althea took her seat, not quite believing the spectacle unfolding before her. A stream, fed by a large catch-bowl, meandered down the middle of the table around huge banks of flowers. Flashes of gold and silver betrayed the presence of fishes swimming in the water.

Her gaze followed the stream to the end of the table—she saw that John was seated there. They exchanged glances. He gave her a brief smile before looking away.

Iron butterflies danced in her stomach.

When soup was served from gargantuan silver tureens, she was unable to swallow it. A lavish meal of roasts, cold dishes, plus mountains of fruit, both in and out of season, followed this. It was accompanied by the appropriate wines and iced champagne offered in copious amounts, but Althea merely toyed with her food and drank very little.

Although she took little interest in what was set before her, Althea did notice that everyone who sat at the prince's table was served their food on silver plates. She mentioned it to Marcus.

Marcus nodded. "You might be interested to know that even the multitude dining outside in the garden are being served their food on silver. I suspect that our host used up every ingot of silver the smiths had at their disposal. I pity anyone setting up house right now. There is bound to be a shortage of silverware for a while."

When the banquet was over, Marcus took Althea aside. "If you have anything to say to my brother, he will be waiting for you in a small room directly opposite the one we were in earlier."

Her heart beat faster.

"I do not mean this unkindly, my dear. I think you would make a fine addition to our family, but please, I beg of you, do not go there unless you have made up your mind to marry him. He has been hurt enough."

"I am sorry for that. I love John and I want to marry him. I was not sure that he loved me in return. Since my come-out I have been subjected to all sorts of indignities."

"I can imagine. You are considered to be the most eligible

young lady to enter Society for many a year. Fortunately, our parents were a love-match and John and I were raised to believe that love is the only reason to get married."

"I think I shall get along with your parents very well." She gave Marcus a shy smile. "You also."

Marcus gave her a bow. "Thank you, Althea. It will make life more pleasant. Now just wait another five minutes before you go, or tongues will be wagging harder than hounds' tails at a foxhunt."

John waited for a slight nod from Marcus, then walked down the corridor to the room that their host had graciously allowed him to use. He found that the room was furnished in the Chinese style, reminiscent of the pavilion at Brighton.

He had been there less than a minute when the door opened. He rushed forward, eager to reconcile with Althea. "I am so glad you came," he said, then stood stock-still.

It was Belinda Vickery who walked through the door and lost no time closing it behind her. "I am happy to hear you say that, John darling," she said in a voice as sweet as Jamaican sugar. "You, too, must realize that a love such as ours cannot be denied."

John stepped back. "I realize nothing of the sort. I rather thought you would have married your rich suitor by now. What was his name?"

Belinda gave a disparaging shrug. "It is of no importance. The man was a charlatan. It turned out that all he owned went down on a ship returning from China. Can you imagine anything so bourgeois? Naturally, my dear papa sent him packing."

"Naturally," John echoed.

Belinda gave a nervous giggle and proceeded to roam the room, picking up and then replacing one treasure after another. Then she came upon a looking glass and she gazed into this until John coughed to get her attention.

She looked surprised to see him, as if she'd been so absorbed with her own image she had forgotten he was there.

"I do not wish to seem unkind, Belinda, but please leave. I am expecting someone else."

Her eyes widened in surprise. "Another girl? That is impossible. I am your true love, and always shall be."

"Belinda, any love you and I might have shared died long ago, and I am not foolish enough to believe that you think otherwise. I suppose it was unsporting of me not to apprise you of the inheritance I was expecting, but there you are."

Her face contorted with rage and it occurred to John that it was probably the first genuine emotion that he had ever seen registered there.

John heard the handle turn in the door and the look of rage on Belinda's face turned to one of indescribable malice. Before he could stop her, she flung her arms around his neck and kissed him soundly on the lips.

He put her from him in time to see Althea standing in the doorway, her face frozen into a mask of horror. John would have sold his soul to the devil to have spared her the torment he saw on her face.

He reached out to her in supplication, but without a word, she turned on her heel and fled the room.

144

Chapter 16

John brushed past Belinda and followed Althea out of the room. He stopped short when he saw that all heads were turned to watch her precipitous flight down the corridor. The last thing he wanted to do was to involve her in a scandal, so he turned around and walked the other way.

The next time he saw her, along with her mother and uncle, she was taking her leave of the prince. John was about to follow her party out to their carriage when Marcus put a restraining hand on his shoulder.

"Let her go, John," he said. "You have done enough damage for one night."

John broke away from his grasp. "But I did nothing wrong. I am sure that if I explain everything to Althea she will understand."

Marcus put a finger over his lips. "Hush. Before you go haring off into the night, we need to talk it over, but not here. Too many people around with their ears pricked for my liking."

He led John to an alcove off another corridor. "This is better." He sat down on a bench covered in rose-colored damask and gestured for John to join him. "Now tell me what took place, and be warned, brother—if I do not care for what I hear, I am likely to call you out myself."

"Belinda Vickery followed me into the room. I am surprised the prince even knows that family exists, much less invited them to this affair. I wonder how they managed it?"

"I know you are searching for ways for it *not* to have happened, but it did and there is nothing you or anyone else can do about it, so you have to take it from there.

"What did the little schemer want?" Marcus put up his

145

hand. "No. Do not say, let me guess—she said that jilting you was not her idea, her parents made her do it, and nothing should stand between a love as great as yours. It is amazing how often a chap coming into a fortune transports some women to heights of hitherto overlooked passion."

"Marcus, I am suffering enough. I do not need you rubbing salt in the wounds. You should have seen the look on her face when I told her that I was waiting for another girl and that she should leave—pure, unmitigated spite."

Marcus groaned. "Small wonder. Words like that could get you gutted like a flounder. Pretty speeches were never your forte."

"You could show a little sympathy. I have just been put through hell."

"Do not expect any sympathy from me, brother. I cannot believe you allowed that shallow little vixen to get the better of you."

John became defensive. "What would you have had me do? I could not very well boot her out, now could I? Force was out of the question. It is just not done."

"No. But the moment she entered the room, you should have left post haste, if not sooner. How could you be so naive? By Jove, I should have thought you would have learned *something* over the years, watching me wriggle out of similar situations. Well, what's done is done. Then what happened?"

"The moment she heard Althea coming in, the little jade flung her arms around my neck and kissed me. It was sheer spite on her part. And to think I almost married that little nightmare! Brrr!"

John slumped down on the seat, feeling utterly dejected. "I suppose you would have foreseen that. You are right. I should have left and no doubt Althea will agree with you."

"Not quite. From my experience, the ladies have a habit of looking at things from a completely different viewpoint."

"Oh?"

"Althea will probably be of the opinion that you did not struggle too hard when Belinda kissed you."

"Are you saying that there is no chance I can convince her to take me back?"

"Not tonight. The hour is late and she will be far too tired to listen to your nonsense. Try again after breakfast. Mind you, I am not saying she will look kindly on your suit. That might take a month of Sundays, but you have to start somewhere."

"That makes sense. I shall call on her tomorrow."

"Good, now go home. Things have a way of looking better after a good night's sleep."

Knowing that most members of the *ton* seldom broke their fast before ten o'clock, John arrived at Camberly House at eleven-thirty to be told by the housekeeper that Lady Camberly and her family had left for her country seat earlier in the morning.

He was tempted to follow her, but not only was a summer storm brewing, he realized it made more sense to return to Fairfax House to collect his servants and carriage and accouterments and start out early the following morning. Having decided this, he reclaimed Orion from the groom and rode away.

On returning to Camberly, John called on Althea several times and she was never "at home" to him. He sent her a letter by courier, and it was returned unopened. One week later, he was standing by his library window, gazing at the towers and turrets of Camberly Hall and feeling thoroughly depressed by the hopelessness of the situation, when Marcus walked in.

John was pleased he came. "Hello. I did not expect to see you. Keeping an eye on me, are you? Making sure I do not make a cake of myself?"

Marcus walked over and gave him a brief hug. "No. I came to discuss something with you."

"Whatever it is, sit down and have a glass of wine with me."

"Thank you, but if it is all the same to you, after riding for several hours I prefer to stand—but I will take that glass of wine. A little fellowship might do you some good. It does not do to mope about."

John looked at his shoes. "Then you guessed that I did not make any headway with Althea?"

"It is very difficult to reconcile with someone who will not even talk to you."

John came to attention. "How did you know that?"

"Just a guess. Why else would you be acting like a hermit? You look as if you haven't eaten a decent meal in days. But enough of that. I have something far more serious to discuss with you."

"Concerning?"

"Our affairs in France. We have suspected for some time that there is a traitor in our midst. A plan gone awry here, an agent missing there."

"Whom do you suspect—my liaison, Bonheur?"

"Not anymore. He has not been seen for a month. We presume that he was taken by the police, in which case he is probably dead. Savary has proved to be far more vigorous in extracting confessions from his victims than was Fouche."

"Let us hope that you are mistaken. He was a good man. I would like to think that he went into hiding."

"If it gives you comfort—but just in case, we are ending this particular endeavour as the risks outweigh the benefits. But we would like to go out in a blaze of glory."

"And what does that entail—or should I be afraid to ask?"

"We thought we would send one more message to Bonheur, implicating some key people both in the police force and the army in seditious activities. Not true, of course, but it should throw the French off-balance for a while."

"Correct me if I am wrong. You expect me to walk right into a trap? You are far too good to me, I must say."

Marcus looked hurt. "Of course not What sort of monster would that make me? From what has transpired, we have come to the conclusion that the French garnered their information from the letters that passed through Celeste Markham's hands—and then, later, Althea's."

John grabbed Marcus by the lapels of his coat "That is a filthy thing to say. How dare you suggest that either one of those fine ladies is capable of betraying their country?"

Marcus held John off. "Steady on there—I do not think that for a minute. It is my opinion that someone at the house made a duplicate of the seal we use. They have been opening our messages, resealing them after reading them, and then you have been giving them to Bonheur and no one has been the wiser."

John pulled back, somewhat mollified. "I suppose that primrose design was too easy to duplicate. Whom do you suspect—the marquis?"

"He is the most likely one—but then it could be his valet, or even that maid of Celeste's. They are both French."

"If Savary did arrest Bonheur, one has to wonder why. Surely he was more useful to them alive?"

"One would think so. Perhaps it was expedience? Savary's performance could have been at an ebb and in need of a boost. Who knows what goes on among those jackals?"

"*Or*—"

"Or what?" John queried.

"Perhaps someone else has taken Bonheur to gain information to further their own career. Someone who wishes Savary to be seen in an unfavorable light."

"And to top it off, you wish me to send one more message through the Markham ladies to set a trap for Savary and his agents? One that you have no intention of being delivered?"

"You have the idea," Marcus replied.

"You must be absolutely mad. From your snug nest in London, all this intrigue must seem quite a lark, but if Bonheur is alive, I am sure he would tell you differently. Marcus, does it not occur to you that these machinations have placed Celeste and Althea in dire peril? *If* Savary, or one of his agents, saw fit to do away with Bonheur, perhaps the ladies are scheduled to be the final sacrifice on the altar of ambition."

"Surely not. I doubt Bonaparte would risk it. Such a deed would bring our revenge down upon the heads of his armies, and for what? Celeste and Althea would no longer be a threat to France."

John threw up his hands. "Marcus, Marcus. How can you be sure that Savary would even consult Bonaparte before acting? Come to think of it, the Marquis de Maligny has an unlikely association with two of the most unsavory characters ever to come out of France."

Marcus stiffened. "Oh? I take it these are people you have met?"

"Not exactly. Althea pointed them out to me that afternoon we spent together on the esplanade. They were going into Hansford's at the time and she thought it odd that they would do so, it being a Sunday. She did tell me the name of the taller of the two, but I am damned if I can remember it. Began with a J. J-J-Joubert, I believe it was."

Marcus gestured. "Never mind that—if they are French agents, I doubt they gave their right names. A good description would be far more useful."

"I saw them but briefly, but Joubert was tall and dark— *saturnine* is the word that comes to mind. His associate was shorter, and rotund—rather jolly-looking, one might say."

"With hair the color and texture of straw," Marcus inserted.

The tone of his voice sounded through John's being like a death knell. "Y-you know of this man, then?"

"Auguste Reston. One of the most cold-blooded assassins and torturers in existence. Savary has the reputation, but it is Reston who does his dirty work for him."

Without a word, John took a highly polished ebony case from a cabinet and removed a pair of Manton pistols from it. He offered one to Marcus but he refused it. "Keep it, I've brought my own." He patted his side.

John's eyes narrowed. "Then I suggest we get to Camberly Hall with all speed. We have to get Althea and her mother away from there. Then, to guarantee their safety, there is nothing for it but we hunt those villains down and kill them."

With that, they dashed out of the library to the rear of the house, the shortest route to the stables, where they hurried the grooms into saddling Orion for John and a fresh mount for Marcus, a large, black hunter named Thunder.

Althea sat on a bench and stared unseeingly into the lily pond. Large, golden carp swam by her in the shadow of the lily pads, but she paid them no heed. Gradually the sound of footsteps crunching on the gravel path impinged upon her consciousness. She looked up to see her mother fast approaching.

On reaching the pool, Celeste sat down beside her and let out a sigh. "That quite took my breath away. The weather is very close today."

"That is why I am sitting here, Mama. It is cooler."

"I quite agree—the willow offers wonderful shade. By the way, there is a letter for you from Philippe. I expect it is to express his undying gratitude for being welcomed back into the fold."

Althea grinned. "Either that, or to thank me for returning his ring. In which case it is his wife's gratitude that should be without end."

Celeste nodded. "I am sure she is pleased with it, but I did not come out here to talk about Philippe's affairs."

The smile left Althea's face. "Please, Mama, if you have come here to talk about John, do not waste your time. As far as I am concerned, there is nothing to discuss."

Celeste shrugged. "Very well. I pity you, Althea. It makes for a very lonely existence to have such little capacity for love and understanding in one's heart."

Althea felt a rising resentment. "Are you suggesting that I overlook his outrageous behavior?"

"No. I am just wondering how you can deny a fair hearing to someone you claim to love. The lowliest prisoner at Newgate gets as much."

"Mama, I was *there*. I *saw* him kiss that girl. He knew I was going to meet him in that room—why would he play such a cruel trick? It was as if he deliberately went out of his way to humiliate me."

Celeste rolled her eyes. "Althea, for an intelligent girl, you can be most obtuse. Think carefully, and tell me exactly what you saw when you entered that room."

"He held her in his arms and was kissing her."

"Where were her arms?"

"Wrapped around his neck. But I fail to see—"

"And his?"

Althea was at a loss. "Holding her close to him, I suppose."

"You *suppose?* Come now, darling, that is not good enough. I want to know exactly where his arms were. Around her waist? Or perhaps he held her firmly between her shoulder blades?"

"I do not recall. Does it really matter?"

"Only if you are interested in justice. Think, child, *think.* You have a clear picture of her arms being entwined around his neck—but where were *his?*"

"On her shoulders. He was grasping her shoulders."

"Althea, a lack of trust turns love into a travesty. John was pushing her *away.* She is Belinda Vickery, the young lady—and I use that term loosely—who jilted John for a man whom she deemed to be more flush in the pocket."

Celeste caught her breath. "To make a long story short, it turned out he was not, and she found out that John *was,* so she saw her family's invitation to Carlton House as an opportunity to woo him back. Naturally, he repudiated the scheming little baggage."

"But they were kissing."

Celeste threw up her hands. "What am I to do with you? He told her he was awaiting the arrival of another young lady. The kiss was for your benefit. An act of pure malice on her part."

Althea wanted to believe that it was so. Not seeing John left her with a hollow feeling. On the other hand, if what her mother said was true, she had not proved to be worthy of his love. Althea felt wretched and yet she needed further reassurance.

"How came you by this knowledge?"

"Jarvis, of course. He and Reeves, the Underhill butler whom John kept on, have been friends for years."

"He does not keep his master's secrets too well."

"The way Jarvis put it, the man has known Mr. Ridley since he was in leading strings and is terribly concerned for his happiness."

Althea was contrite. "You are right, Mama, I have treated John dreadfully. I feel so unworthy, so thoroughly lacking in compassion. How could I have been so wrapped up in myself, so—"

"Althea, stop it this instant! You are absolutely wallowing. No one should be allowed that much pleasure."

"What do I do now? Dash right over to Seacliff, or send a footman there with a letter asking his forgiveness?"

Celeste patted her hand. "A letter will do nicely, but practice restraint. None of that sackcloth and ashes nonsense—it does not do to let a gentleman get the upper hand. Just let him know that you are willing to listen to his explanation, and then, after careful consideration, say you will forgive him. After all, you are not entirely to blame. I am of the opinion that he could have handled the situation far better."

"Would you help me write it, Mama? I should be most terribly grateful if you would."

Celeste rose from the bench and smoothed her skirt. "Of course, darling. If we get right to it, this whole misunderstanding can be settled by morning."

They returned to the house with arms linked, Althea responding to her mother's humor with outbursts of delighted laughter.

When they reached Althea's private sitting room, she pulled an extra chair up to a small rosewood escritoire in front of the window and urged her mother to sit down. Althea sat beside her, removed a quill from the inkstand, and turned to face her, a look of anticipation on her face.

"Well, Mama, how should I start?"

Before she could answer, Lizzie opened the connetting door to Althea's dressing room and poked her head around. "I thought I heard voices. I was just sorting through your things, madam. I can come back later, if you like."

"No, go right ahead, Lizzie. You might want to inspect the dress I wore to dinner last evening. I believe I had a mishap with some wine. White wine, fortunately."

"I have already attended to it."

She closed the door once more and Althea and Celeste exchanged smiles. Lizzie had sounded enormously pleased with her own efficiency.

Althea put the quill in the inkstand and turned to her mother once more. "Well, Mama, how should I address him? Should it be 'My dear Mr. Ridley' or 'My dearest John'?"

Celeste laughed. "Mr. Ridley, of course. Otherwise, he will know he has been forgiven. You must not make it too easy for him—gentlemen sometimes take it as a sign that they may get into all sorts of mischief with impunity. One must begin as one means to go on."

"In that case," Althea rejoined, "I shall accord him a mere, 'Dear Mr. Ridley.' I should not like him to think that I lay claim to his affections."

"Brava. You will do beautifully."

Before Althea could put pen to paper, there was a knock at the door. "Botheration," she muttered, returned the quill to the inkstand, and got up to see who was there.

She expected to see Jarvis on the other side, with some footling complaint regarding below-stairs intrigue, but to her surprise she found her uncle at the door with Monsieur Joubert and—what was his friend's name? She could not remember. Both were hovering at his shoulder, and in light of the warm weather, both were even more sorely in need of a bath than the last time they came to Camberly Hall.

Althea gave the marquis a questioning look.

The marquis lowered his gaze and cleared his throat. "These, er—gentlemen are desirous of an audience with you, niece."

Althea narrowed her nostrils to alleviate the stench emanating from the hall. "Kindly inform your, er—friends that it is inconvenient for the present."

He gave her a look that bespoke of abject misery. "Please do not be difficult, I *implore* you."

Before Althea could reply, Monsieur Joubert pushed the marquis into the room. The shorter man followed close behind, taking care to close the door behind him.

Celeste put herself between Althea and the intruders.

"What is the meaning of this outrage?" she demanded.

"Hold your tongue, madam," the shorter man replied softly. "Nothing would give me greater pleasure than to strike your

154

pampered, aristocratic face."

"*Please,* you swore on your honor that no harm would befall my nieces."

"Spoken like an *aristo.* Only your kind can afford the luxury of honor."

He turned to his associate. "Listen to the fool, Joubert. He thinks that keeping his word is somehow more important than treating the common people in a decent and humane manner." He spat on the carpet. "This is what I think of your honor."

Althea moved forward. "That is quite enough. Leave my uncle alone. You did not come here to spout your egalitarian rhetoric. You want something from me, so tell me what it is and have done with it."

The man gave her a look of pure hatred. "I am thinking that before this day is over, madam, you will have lost some of your arrogance. But you are right, I do want something from you, and if not from you, then your mother."

"You seem to be in charge and I have forgotten your name, monsieur. Before we go any further, perhaps you should refresh my memory," Althea said.

"My name is Reston. Auguste Reston."

"Hmm. That does not sound familiar."

"That is because it is not the name he went by," the marquis interjected. "Forgive me, Althea, I had no idea. Auguste Reston is the most ruthless man in all of France. He is known to derive great pleasure from torturing secrets out of those who fall into his hands. In fact, it is said that he is disappointed if his victims break too soon."

Reston bowed. "Just so we understand one another."

Before more words could be exchanged, there was another knock on the door.

"It is probably my housekeeper," Althea whispered. "She sometimes comes to confer with me this time of day." Reston pushed Althea forward. "Get rid of her. If you try to warn her in any way, I shall be forced to kill her."

Althea decided it would be safer not to even open the door. "Who is it?" she called out.

"Mrs. Denchforth, my lady. I was wondering if I could have a few minutes of your time."

"I shall send for you later, Mrs. Denchforth. I am in the middle of writing a very important letter."

It occurred to Althea that in all probability she might not get to finish the letter. Her scalp tightened at the thought. Then it occurred to her that perhaps John was the only chance that any of them had of getting out of this predicament alive.

"You handled that very well," Reston said. "I am glad you decided to be sensible. I take no pleasure in killing innocent peasants."

Althea raised her voice, hoping that Lizzie would take heed. "Neither do I, Monsieur Reston. I would not want any of my servants put at risk. Mark my words, if my friend, Mr. *Soames* were here, that would be another matter entirely. Mr. *Soames* would put you in your place."

"Do not waste my time with your silly bravado. By now you should know better. You and this red-haired devil who gave birth to you are enemies of France. You plot to bring about the downfall of our republic."

"What made you suspect us?" Celeste asked.

"Joubert and I saw you in Paris. I was struck by your beauty and the fiery color of your hair. I thought to while away a night or two in your company, but the street was crowded and I lost sight of you. Further inquiry did not shed any light as to your whereabouts, or indeed, if you had ever existed. Imagine my surprise when your fool of an uncle presented me to you. There was no doubt in my mind that the French peasant and the Dowager Countess of Camberly were one and the same."

Celeste's eyes flashed scorn. "While away a night or two with you? Pah! We have pigs who smell sweeter."

Reston smiled. "Do not hold back your venom, dear lady. Later, you will pay for every syllable." He turned to Althea. "Sad to say, but I am of the opinion that you are both very difficult women."

Althea shrugged.

"I am thinking that it will take a lot of persuasion on my

part to get either one of you to tell me what I want to know. Therefore we shall continue this interview in a place where we are less likely to be disturbed."

"That would be Hansford's, the linen drapers? Good—perhaps he has some fresh laces in stock."

"For pity's sake, Althea, are you quite mad?" her uncle wailed. "Do not play games with Monsieur Reston. Just tell him what he wants to know. He will get it from you eventually."

"You would do well to follow his advice."

"Tell me, Uncle. How did you manage to get involved with these two?"

"I was promised that if I kept them informed of what was taking place within emigre circles, my estate in France would be restored to me. I had Bonaparte's word on that."

Reston laughed. "You gullible old fool, how you babble—'word,' this, 'honor,' that. Bonaparte does not even know of your existence."

The marquis seemed to shrivel.

Althea turned on him, feeling nothing but scorn for him. "You would spy on your own flesh and blood? Have you no heart?"

His eyes welled with tears. "I was given two options. Cooperate, and your lives would be spared. Otherwise..." He threw up his hands in despair.

"Either this maudlin drivel ends *now,* or you will suffer the consequences. Enough is enough," Reston interjected.

"What more can he do to us?" Althea muttered under her breath. "We are as good as dead as it is."

"What did you say?"

"Nothing you would care to hear, Monsieur. Just a few Anglo-Saxon epithets questioning your parentage."

He grabbed her jaw and stared into her eyes. His breath bespoke teeth in various stages of putrefaction. "It is *Citizen* Reston. I scorn all bourgeois titles."

"I find that strange, Citizen. Your hygiene might leave much to be desired, but your English is flawless, your accent as well-bred as any member of the *ton.* I suspect the same might be said of your French."

"It is none of your concern, but I shall satisfy your curiosity anyway. I sometimes indulge the condemned. My father owned a boys' school not too far from Paris. St. Françoise by name. My mother was an English governess whom he met quite by accident when the family she worked for was touring France. They both believed that education was best applied with the use of the birch. They achieved their goal. I know an inordinate amount about the most inconsequential matters, and bear the scars to prove it. As for you, madam, be warned. You will pay for your impudence. By the time I have finished with you, you will find little humor in your situation. I, on the other hand…"

On first encounter, Althea had thought him to be such a jolly-looking man but today she had seen expressions on his face of such malevolence, she was surprised that they had not all turned to stone.

"I want you to listen very carefully. The lives of some of your servants may depend on your following my instructions to the letter."

"I understand."

"You will summon your butler and arrange for three horses to be saddled for you. When they are ready, we shall go downstairs. We will laugh and talk as if we are all having a—how do the English put it? Ah, yes, as if we are all having a jolly good time. Do not try to be clever, or someone is bound to get hurt."

"I give you the word of an English gentlewoman. Contrary to what you might think, it is possible to value one's honor while at the same time care for the welfare of those in one's service."

"Pah! Sanctimonious claptrap. Just follow my orders, then, as you guessed, we shall ride over to Hansford's."

"I understand."

While waiting for Jarvis to answer her summons, Althea decided to question Reston further. There was always the possibility that they might survive the ordeal, in which case, any information she might get out of him could prove useful.

"Tell me, Citizen Reston, what sort of person is your superior, Citizen Savary? Is he as clever as they say?"

"Pah! He is a carrion crow."

"Oh?"

"He feeds on others and sucks their bones dry."

"I do not understand."

"It is simple enough. He plots and schemes and takes the credit for the accomplishments of his subordinates. He has climbed to where he is at the expense of better men."

"But you will get the better of him, will you not? You are far too intelligent to let him use you twice."

"You have the right of it. For instance, he has no idea that I have uncovered your nest of vipers—and shall not in time to do himself any good."

"You play a clever game."

"Be quiet. You are beginning to bore me."

With every step she took, she prayed that Lizzie had stayed in the dressing room long enough to hear what had transpired. It occurred to her that with the threat of death hanging over her head, it was the thought of dying without having reconciled with John that gave her the most trouble.

Chapter 17

John and Marcus pounded on the door to Camberly Hall, each compelled by a feeling that he had not a moment to lose. Jarvis, apparently affronted by their lack of decorum, admitted them with a disapproving sniff.

Knowing that his brother was not being received by Althea, Marcus spoke for both of them.

"Good afternoon, Jarvis. We have come to see your mistress on a matter of the utmost importance."

"I am sorry, your lordship, but you just missed Lady Camberly, I fear."

"The older Lady Camberly, then? The situation is really grave, else I would not persist."

"I do not doubt it, sir, but they left together. They rode off with his lordship and those two French acquaintances of his."

"Tell me, Jarvis, do you happen to know if they were going to the village?"

"If they were going into Camberly, surely you would have passed them?"

"Not if they cut through the fields."

John groaned. "I have a bad feeling about this."

Suddenly their attention was caught by the sound of a horse approaching. They turned to see Lizzie coming from the direction of the stables, riding a dun-colored mare.

She slipped from the saddle and rushed over and bobbed to them. "Thank goodness you are here. I had the devil's own time convincing someone at the stable to saddle a horse for me. I was just on my way to get you, Mr. Ridley."

John grabbed her by the shoulders. "Just tell me where they are taking them—that is, if you know."

"Hansford's on the esplanade, if you can believe it, sir."

"I should have known," John said grimly.

Without another word, the brothers retrieved their horses and took off for Camberly with all speed.

They rode in silence for the first mile, then Marcus said, "How are we going about this? After all, we have to have some sort of plan."

"That would depend on the circumstances, would it not? I mean to say, we cannot just storm the place. This Reston chap is liable to shoot the three of them just for the pleasure of it."

"I quite agree. Treat it like a military exercise. Reconnoiter and go in as soon as we see an opening. That is, unless…"

John turned sharply in his saddle. "Unless? What is that supposed to mean?"

"Steady on, John. We have to face the fact that Althea and Celeste are at the mercy of one of the most depraved beasts of our age. Mind you, he will keep them alive so long as they are useful to him—but at what price? There might come a point when risk outweighs prudence."

"That has been on my mind since we left Camberly Hall," John said. "That is not something one can plan ahead. Circumstances are sometimes the deciding factor."

"Very well," said Marcus, "then it is agreed that we have to remain flexible?"

"I see no other way."

By the time they reached the esplanade it was getting close to evening. The only place open for business was The Boar's Head and only a few stragglers were to be seen strolling about.

John's gaze strayed toward the harbor. The boat that had been home to him for so long was moored there. "See that Fennimore has *The Seafoam* out there. Wonder what he is doing here. You would not happen to know, would you?"

Marcus grinned. "Hear he has an itch for the little tavern maid. You must admit she is a toothsome little morsel."

"She is also far too young to know what she is doing."

Marcus laughed. "I think she has a fairly good idea. In any case, one can safely presume that the captain will be spending tonight at The Boar's Head."

When they neared Hansford's, fearing the sound of their horses' hooves would alert Reston of their presence, John approached a youth whom he recognized as a local and offered him a shilling to mind their horses. Promised a sovereign on their return, he agreed with alacrity.

The living quarters had to be to the rear of the shop, so they entered the side gate leading to the back garden. A horse neighed. It was the plaintive sound a horse makes while waiting to be fed.

"Dammit," Marcus whispered. "I hope Reston does not decide to feed that beast."

"I hope he does," John whispered back. "If we can divide, we can also conquer."

"That would be too much to hope for. Besides, I am sure that with two helpless women at his mercy, a complaining horse would not even register with him."

John felt the hairs on his arms stiffen. "If that swine so much as lays a hand on them, I swear I will tear him apart with my bare hands."

At this point they had reached the back garden. In spite of the stables boasting a small paddock, it was a sorry-looking affair. Next to this was a privy made of weathered boards. The garden proper was comprised of cracked flagstones bordered with weed-choked flowerbeds.

As they had surmised, the living quarters faced the neglected garden and to the right a scullery jutted out to form an ell. Marcus tried the latch to this and found it was open.

"Obliging of them," he whispered.

John gestured to a window to the left of the scullery. "Better take a look first. See how everyone is situated."

Marcus nodded, and they tiptoed over and crouched under the window. A quick glance showed that Reston held Celeste firmly by the arm while Joubert was in the process of tying Althea to a chair. The marquis stood next to the fireplace, a hangdog expression on his face.

"This is completely unnecessary," Althea said. "I gave you

the name of our liaison and I am perfectly willing
everything he told me about *his* associates on the con
has several, you know."

"Shut up and sit still," Reston replied, his soft voice b
the menace it carried. "Even a child would not believe that
story you concocted. A Corsair pirate ship sailing up the Camb
estuary, indeed."

"The brave little thing is trying to stretch it out in the hope
that I'll rescue her in time," John said, "but she is no match
for Reston."

"Do as Citizen Reston tells you," Joubert said. "It will
make my job a lot easier, although I must admit it is much more
interesting when a prisoner struggles." He lowered his voice.
"Especially a pretty one. We shall have fun with these two later
on—*non*?" He ran a caressing hand the length of Althea's throat.

"Non," Celeste screamed. She broke free from Reston and
landed a kick on Joubert's behind, which sent him sprawling.
Reston retaliated by striking Celeste on the face.

With pistol in hand, John made a dash for the scullery
door, Marcus following close behind. When they came though
the door to the main room, Reston was waiting for them, pistol
cocked. John stopped short and aimed his own pistol, but
Reston had the advantage. His finger curled around the trigger
and squeezed. There was a loud report.

John fully expected to be hit but to his amazement it was
the marquis who lay at Reston's feet. The man had taken the
shot for him.

John had a clear aim at Reston's heart, but at the last minute,
he lowered his pistol and aimed for his kneecap instead. Howling
in pain, Reston toppled like a ninepin.

Seeing that his brother had his pistol aimed at Joubert, John
hastened to inspect the marquis's wound. He was relieved to
see that he had only sustained a grazed shoulder. John stuffed
a handkerchief inside the old gentleman's shirt and led him to
a chair.

Joubert threw down his pistol and raised his hands in
surrender. Evidently still enraged by the threat he had imposed

ewe lamb, Celeste kicked him once more. He joined the floor, clutching his manhood and, if possible, g even louder than his partner.

arcus winced. "Tut, tut, my dear, that was scarcely cricket."

Celeste shrugged. "No. I think it is called revenge, and in se you are interested, it *is* sweet. *Very, very,* sweet."

"I am glad to hear it." He looked askance at the two men writhing on the floor. "Must you make that noise? You sound like a couple of pigs on slaughtering day."

"Would someone take the trouble to untie me?" Althea interjected. "I am losing the feeling in my hands."

Once freed, she ran to her uncle's side. "I pray that your wound is not too severe?"

He brushed her away. "It is nothing, more's the pity. It would have been far better had I died. I most assuredly deserved to."

"I will not have you say that. You were incredibly brave."

"Brave? Thanks to me, you and your mother almost suffered the most horrible of deaths."

"See here, sir," John interjected. "You might not always make wise choices, but as far as I am concerned, you more than proved your nobility. Every single day, for as long as I live, I shall remember that you were willing to die for me."

Reston chose that moment to utter a loud moan and Althea saw that he was losing a lot of blood. "For pity's sake, if he is to live, we had better stanch his wound."

She tore a strip off her petticoat and looked to John. "Do you have a knife?"

He nodded.

She handed him the torn strip. "Then cut his trouser leg and use this for a tourniquet while he still has some blood in him."

Afterwards, they left their prisoners in the local gaol, with strict orders for the gaoler to summon a doctor to see to Reston's injury.

"An exercise in futility, really," Marcus said. "As soon as they have been thoroughly questioned, they will be executed, of course."

They escorted the ladies and the marquis safely back to

Camberly Hall. While Lizzie and Colette swept their mistresses upstairs, clucking and fussing over them like mother hens taking their chicks on their first outing, Marcus and John took the marquis off to the library for a chat.

Once they were seated and sipping the marquis's cognac, which in a rare fit of generosity he invited them to share, Marcus brought up the matter of the former's culpability in the affair.

"You realize, of course, that the authorities have to be told."

The older man sighed. "I am aware of that. If I wait for them to wring it out of Reston and Joubert, it will only go the worse for me."

"I am dreadfully sorry, sir. If it were up to me, I would let you go."

The marquis looked wry. "Do not concern yourself. I would not be in this predicament had I not put worldly things before my honor."

"We all make mistakes. I think you more than atoned for yours," Marcus said.

The marquis shrugged. "It would appear that the devil knows the asking price of every man's soul. In my case, it was getting my old life back. According to Reston, all I had to do was keep him informed as to the movements of my fellow exiles and Bonaparte would restore my beloved Avencon to me." He laughed. It was a hollow sound without a trace of mirth to it. "It was a complete fabrication on his part. Bonaparte had no hand in this."

"Far be it from me to judge you. It must be hard to reconcile losing everything that defines one's place in the world. I like to think that under the same circumstances I would do the right thing—but who knows?"

The marquis sighed. "You are far too charitable Lord Ridley. There is no excuse for my behavior, and you know it My honor was the one thing of any value that I could still call my own. How ironic that I would give it up of my own accord on the strength of the idle promises of a rogue."

"See here, sir," John interjected. "You might have lost sight of it momentarily, but in the final analysis it was your sense of honor that helped save all of our lives."

The marquis shook his head. "One could think so, but I know better. My niece, Celeste, once said that we de Malignys are a dreadful lot. In my case, that is true. I took that shot for my sake, not for yours. I am sorry to disillusion you, sir, but saving you was the last thought on my mind."

John leaned forward. "Are you saying you were *trying* to get killed?"

"Not exactly. The gallantry my nieces displayed in the face of certain death reminded me of what it meant to be a de Maligny. Were they not magnificent?"

John nodded. "I knew that of the older Lady Camberly almost from the moment we met. I would expect no less of her daughter."

The marquis gestured impatiently. "Do you not see? Under the circumstances, my hand was forced—there was nothing for it but that I rise to the occasion."

He was silent for a moment, then erupted into a short laugh. "Come to think of it, my pathetic little show of bravery was in itself a manifestation of cowardice."

John emptied his glass, placed it on a tray atop a small walnut table, and stood up. The marquis's descent into self-loathing had become far too painful for him to witness. Marcus quickly followed suit.

"Come, sir," John said. "You are being far too hard on yourself. Any soldier will tell you that the greatest acts of bravery during battle are brought about by such fears."

The marquis held up his hand. "No more. I appreciate your kindness, but it is to no avail. I violated my own standards. The worst part is the consequences I have brought down on the head of my grandson, Philippe. The poor boy must also suffer the shame I have brought upon the de Maligny name."

Marcus put a comforting hand on his shoulder. "I shall speak to the authorities on your behalf. I have the ear of the Prince Regent—his influence might be brought to bear on your part in this."

"Naturally, I would be most grateful for anything you can

do to mitigate the damage I have done. I sincerely hope you do not withdraw your friendship from my nieces because of my misdeeds."

"Rest assured, our friendship for them is in no way impaired." Marcus held out his hand. "Or for you, sir. And I know my parents will agree. Regardless of your culpability, the Ridley family will always be grateful to you for saving John's life."

Seeing that the old gentleman was hard-put to hold back his tears, John and Marcus took their leave of him. Once out of earshot, John said, "Phew, that was getting rather sticky."

"I quite agree. The marquis has suffered enough humiliation for one day without breaking down in front of comparative strangers. I think even the French would draw the line at that."

At seven the next morning, John and Marcus were awakened from a well-earned rest by their respective valets and informed that Squire Collins, the local magistrate, was in the library waiting to speak to them.

John and Marcus stumbled into one another on the landing.

"Damnation," Marcus muttered. "Bunch of incompetents. What could be so difficult about keeping two prisoners under lock and key—one of them wounded at that?"

"Perhaps he has come to tell us that Reston has taken a turn for the worse."

"This early in the morning? I would hardly think so."

"Then we should waste no more time in idle speculation. Let's get to the library and listen to what Collins has to say."

Chapter 18

Later the same morning, Althea and Celeste were about to take a turn around the gardens when they encountered Marcus and John being admitted into the entrance hall by Jarvis.

They exchanged greetings. John smiled, and Althea's lips tingled at the remembrance of the kisses they had shared. To cover her embarrassment at harboring such an immodest thought, she hastily offered her guests the hospitality of the small reception room.

Marcus declined. "If it is all the same to you, John and I would far rather accompany you both on your morning constitutional."

When they came to the lily pond, Marcus motioned them toward the bench. "Please sit down. This should be far enough out of earshot."

"Then I am correct in thinking that this is not a social call?" Celeste asked.

Marcus nodded.

Celeste put a hand to her throat "Then it is as I feared— those monsters have escaped! You should have killed them when you had the opportunity. If anything should happen to Althea—"

"Calm down, dear lady," John interjected. "Those villains are in no position to harm anyone. The gaoler found both of them dead when he went to give them their breakfast this morning."

"But how could that be?" Althea inserted. "Reston's wound was in no way fatal and I fail to see how the—er, retribution Mama exacted upon Joubert's person could have caused his demise."

"You are correct on both points, Althea," Marcus said.

"This would be a good time to interject a word of caution on the subject. Should you, or any member of your household, meet with an accident involving even the slightest amount of blood loss, on no account call upon the services of your local doctor. Reston died because that fool parted him from whatever was left of his blood."

"But what of Joubert?"

"He was beaten to death by a couple of drunken fishermen who were put in his cell later on in the evening. He was foolish enough to complain that the noise they made disturbed his sleep."

Althea was aghast. "And for that, they took his life?"

"Not quite," Marcus replied. "His French accent was his downfall. It seems that both men had lost a brother at the Battle of Trafalgar."

Althea shook her head. "Those drunken fools. Now they have managed to heap more sorrow upon the heads of their families."

Celeste laughed nervously. "I had better watch my step when walking about Camberly."

Althea put a comforting arm around her shoulders. "You have nothing to fear, Mama. The village people love you. Besides, your English is flawless—you do not have the slightest trace of a French accent."

"You are missing the point," Marcus said. "Joubert and Reston are dead, therefore cannot implicate your uncle in this matter. I am sure that for your sake, Celeste, the Prince Regent will use his influence to see that your uncle's part in this intrigue is not mentioned. His Royal Highness is well aware of your role in our effort to bring about the downfall of Bonaparte's government—and greatly admires you for it."

Celeste glowed with pleasure. "I am grateful for his gracious condescension."

"It is well earned," Marcus rejoined. He stood up, and the others followed his lead. "That about covers it, I should think. As soon as this incident has been resolved by the powers that be, you will be hearing from me."

Althea held out her hand. "We are most obliged to you, Marcus. Your news will afford our uncle great comfort. He is really torn up by the guilt and shame."

"Pray do not tell him," Celeste said. "It will do the old rapscallion good to suffer for a while."

"But Mama," Althea remonstrated, "how could you be so heartless?"

"Very easily. Do not forget, my darling, that I, too, am very much a de Maligny." As she said this, she linked arms with Marcus. They walked back to the house, drowning out the birdsong with their chatter and laughter. John and Althea trailed behind them, the awkward silence that hung between them a stark contrast.

Althea and Celeste watched the brothers ride away.

"It seems that is all I ever do," Althea murmured.

"What might that be, darling?"

"Watch John Ridley ride out of my life."

Celeste rolled her eyes. "And whose fault might that be, do you suppose? You must be the most difficult young lady to court in all of England."

Althea sighed. "I know that, Mama. I wish it were otherwise. What do you suppose is wrong with me?"

"Foolish pride. Lack of trust. A feeling deep inside that no one on earth could possibly love you for yourself, and not chancing that it might be otherwise. Would you like me to continue?"

"No, Mama. I think that is enough."

Celeste looked rueful. "Forgive me, darling. I should think before I speak."

"You only spoke the truth. I am a very puzzling creature."

Celeste put her arm around Althea. "One that I happen to love very, very much."

Althea laid her head upon her mother's shoulder, and kept it there until John and Marcus disappeared from view.

• • • •

After an eventful morning, the brothers found returning to Seacliff something of an anticlimax. After lunch, they read for a while, then Marcus cast aside the book he was reading.

"Good heavens, John, how do you stand it?"

"What are you talking about?"

"This life. I have half a mind to return to London. There is to be a masque taking place at the Vauxhall Gardens later in the week that is supposed to be all the crack. Care to come along?"

John looked askance. "Thank you, no. I happen to like it here."

Later in the afternoon the sun came out, casting a shower of diamonds over the sea. Unable to resist the sparkling water, the brothers discarded their clothes in favor of heavy cotton robes and then leaped from terrace to terrace to the beach like a couple of exuberant schoolboys. Here, they threw off their cotton robes and ran naked into the water.

"So much for your Vauxhall Gardens," John called out. "I will race you out to the rock."

"Why do you bother? You have yet to win."

John laughed. "One day your dissolute life is bound to catch up with you and I intend to be there when it happens."

"By then you will be too rusty to move. See you anon, young sprout."

With that, Marcus sliced through the waves with firm, rhythmic strokes, reaching the rock several yards ahead of John. After expending that first burst of energy, they were content to alternate between riding the waves and basking in the water like seals.

As Marcus floated on his back, he became so relaxed his eyes closed. John slapped a spray of water into his face. "Wake up, sleepyhead, it is time to go."

Marcus gave a start. "Good Lord, John, will you ever grow up? Must you persist in playing the aggravating brat?"

John grinned. "Brings back memories of the good old days, does it not? Only now, Aunt Gertrude is no longer here to give us hot chocolate when we return to the house."

"Nothing ever stays the same," Marcus replied. "Nor should

you expect it to. Come on. You are right—we have stayed out here long enough. It's getting cold."

On returning to their chambers, both kept the servants hopping, furnishing them with ever more buckets of hot water as they indulged in long, leisurely baths. Then they went down to dinner, glowing from their afternoon in the sun.

The cook had prepared a particularly succulent roast of beef served with fresh vegetables from the kitchen garden, but John ate very little. Afterwards, he absently twirled his cognac around the sides of the goblet while gazing morosely into a candle flame.

Finally, Marcus put down his cigar and thumped the table with his fist. "For goodness' sake, John, marry the girl and have done with it."

John scowled. "Go ahead, rub salt in the wound if it gives you pleasure. I would marry her tonight, if she would have me. I even took the trouble to procure a special license lest the occasion should arise."

Marcus raised a brow. "Did you indeed? A trifle presumptuous of you, was it not?"

John felt sheepish. "Picked it up when she agreed to meet with me at the prince's fete. Had every intention of talking her into a whirlwind courtship. Damned silly of me, eh?"

"Not at all. Dashed romantic, in fact. As was rushing to her rescue. Knight in shining armor sort of thing. John, old chap, you could not choose a more advantageous time to ask for her hand. Let me tell you what I have in mind…"

Althea spent the rest of the day moping around her private quarters. The day before, when John had departed without claiming her, she had harbored the faint hope that perhaps he was waiting for a more appropriate time to do so. Today, it had seemed to her that his attitude toward her had been cold and impersonal.

Why, he scarcely spoke to me. But who can blame him? I am so puffed up with foolish pride.

When Lizzie came in to help her dress for dinner she waved her away, opting to eat a light supper in her room while waiting for the water to be heated for her bath.

After Lizzie helped her into the bath, Althea dismissed her, saying she would call when she needed her help. As she soaked in the warm water, her mind quieted and a delicious languor, which she finally recognized as a longing to be held and kissed by John, seeped over her body.

When you rescued me yesterday, why, oh, why did you not hold me close and refuse to let me go until I promised to marry you? Am I so dreadful—or is love so fickle? Perhaps you never really loved me.

No longer wishing to dwell on the matter, Althea called for Lizzie. She quietly submitted to having her hair washed, then stood up while Lizzie rinsed her off with fresh water.

Once Althea was toweled dry, Lizzie selected a nightgown of a fine cotton weave for her, but Althea shook her head. "No, Lizzie, tonight I shall wear the silk with all the lace."

"But that was meant for your trousseau."

Althea gave her a wry smile. "In the meantime, no one is banging on the door begging for my hand in marriage. It is liable to rot in the chest first. Besides, it can be replaced, you know."

"I suppose so. If you don't mind me saying, you *are* in a strange mood this evening. There's a full moon out. Perhaps that's why."

"Perhaps."

Lizzie brushed Althea's hair until it crackled, then went to put a lace cap on her head. Althea refused it.

"It is too warm for that."

"Very well," Lizzie huffed. "Don't blame me when all your lovely hair breaks off."

Before their conversation could deteriorate further, Celeste walked in. She also was bathed and ready for bed.

"Finished, Lizzie? Good. Go along with you, my dear, I wish to share the beautiful moon with my little girl."

Once Lizzie left, mother and daughter stood in front of the window and stared outside. The moonlight gave the garden a magical, otherworldly look.

"It is so good to be standing here with you, Mama. For a while there yesterday, I truly thought I would never see the moonlight again."

Celeste squeezed her hand and did not let go. "I had similar thoughts. Every time I think of that ogre, Reston, I shudder. I am not in the least bit sorry that he is dead."

"Neither am I. The brute absolutely terrified me."

"And yet when you stood up to him you seemed absolutely fearless."

"I knew that he would do with me as he wished regardless of how I behaved, so I was bound and determined not to let him see me grovel."

"You are truly a great lady in every sense of the word, my daughter."

Althea smiled. "I must take after you. If you had not kicked that Joubert creature on his derriere, I fear that the outcome might have been different."

"No, the credit for saving us has to go to Uncle Jean-Claude. Who would have thought that he could be so selfless?"

"I think, Mama, that it was a case of your actions reminding him of what is expected of a gentleman. He had just forgotten for a while."

"I suppose I resent the fact that he took his time doing it. I would rather you had been spared that terrible ordeal."

"He is old. He did what he could. My greatest fear was that I had lost my chance to be a wife and mother."

Celeste squeezed her shoulder. "Of course it would be, darling. It is only natural."

Althea leaned into her mother. "Mama, if I cannot marry John, I do not wish to be married at all."

"I am sure that with a little encouragement on your part he will come around. I caught him looking at you once or twice this morning. He is absolutely besotted with you."

"I should hardly think so."

Celeste nudged Althea's arm. "Think again, my doubting Thomasina. Look over there and tell me what you see."

"Where?"

"By the river, of course."

"A lantern. I see it. Smugglers, do you think?"

"One of your Corsair pirates, no doubt. No, my little pea-goose, only one man I know waves a lantern in that particular fashion."

"John! It has to be." Althea wrinkled her brow. "What do you suppose he wants?"

Celeste laughed. "Not *what*. *Who*. John has come for you!"

"But it will take ages for me to get dressed—then there is my hair. By the time I reach the river he will be long gone."

"Nonsense. I can twist your hair and secure it with some combs. Then all you have to do is cover your nightrail with a cloak, accept his offer of marriage, seal the bargain with a lovely kiss, pop back to the house, and he will be none the wiser. He can return tomorrow to iron out the wedding arrangements."

"You are making my head spin."

True to her promise, with a few deft movements, Celeste fixed Althea's hair and handed her a looking glass. "See?" she said. "I told you I could do it."

"Yes, you did. It looks deceptively fine."

She went to her wardrobe and took out a dark blue cloak. Celeste followed her and replaced it with a rose-colored one.

"Yes," she said, sounding well pleased with herself. "It looks perfect and so do you, my little cabbage. Now run along—no, wait."

She dashed into Althea's dressing room. Althea heard the clink of glass being moved around and surmised that her mother was fumbling in the dark, looking for something on her dressing table. A moment or two later she emerged, triumphantly waving a bottle of perfume.

"Found it. A lady should not receive an offer of marriage without wearing an absolutely heavenly scent. Thereafter, when she wears what she considers to be her special perfume, her husband remembers that night and the passion of his youth is rekindled."

Althea felt the heat rise to her face. "Mama, must you always be so relendessly French?"

Celeste tweaked her nose. "Until the day I die, *chérie*. Now stand still while I dab it on you. Let me see, the ear lobes, your throat, your wrists, the backs of your knees."

"The backs of my knees? Is that not a little excessive?"

Celeste smiled. "I rather expect so. Ah! That magical blend of roses and jasmine suits you perfectly."

Celeste enveloped her in an embrace and kissed her on both cheeks. "Now put aside all doubt and fear, my darling, and go to John. With him by your side, you will have a good life."

As Althea sped along the garden path, she could feel the gravel through the soles of her slippers. Her cloak flew open and she looked down and saw that the silk of her nigh trail flowed with the rhythm of each step and shimmered like liquid silver in the moonlight.

Without breaking a step, she pulled the cloak about her, wishing she had not paid attention to her mother's assurances that John would be none the wiser.

I should have known better than to listen to Mama. She has no sense of propriety. If I am not careful, John will regard my shocking state of undress with disgust and loathing and go away in that little dory as fast as his arms can row. Perhaps I should turn around. He is bound to come calling in the morning. No. No. I want that lovely kiss Mama spoke of, here and now.

These thoughts played over and over in Althea's mind. She was tempted to turn back several times, but the passion that comes with young love overrode her doubts.

Through a break in the shrubbery, she saw the glow of John's lantern and, with an extra spurt, she was standing before him, her heart beating as fast as hummingbird wings.

He put an arm around her and shone the lantern in her face. "Just wanted to make sure it was you and not some faerie creature before I kissed you. I do not want to risk losing you ever again."

She wrinkled her nose. "What would you have done if I had failed to see your signal? Sailed away never to return?"

He grinned. "It occurred to me that you might not see my signal. I planned on knocking on your door, but it would have been a complete anticlimax. But enough of that."

He put the lantern down and enveloped her in both arms and kissed her. It was soft and gentle. To Althea it was welcoming her into a place that was safe and warm, somewhere where she would be loved and cherished. So different from the nightmare world she had glimpsed the day before.

She entwined her arms around his neck and deepened the kiss of her own accord. John held her closer. She tasted his essence and instinctively knew that no other man's kisses would taste like John's. No other man's kisses would ever suffice.

Suddenly he scooped her up into his arms and started to carry her toward the riverbank. Althea panicked. This was not the way her mother had said it would be.

"Stop!" she shrieked. "Put me down. What on earth do you think you are doing?"

"Taking you aboard *The Seafoam,* of course." He stood her on her feet. "This can go no further until we do."

Althea straightened her spine. "It was foolish of me to dash out here just because you waved a lamp at me. Even more so for not taking the time to get suitably dressed, but that does not mean that I will allow you to take liberties with my person."

His face registered pure surprise. "I never thought it did. It is because of that that I was taking you to *The Seafoam.* The captain is waiting to marry us. Did I not mention it?"

"No. And whatever gave you the idea that I would consent to spend my wedding night in such close proximity to the captain and his crew?"

"Whatever gave you the idea I would want you to? By the time we have exchanged our vows, *The Seafoam* will have reached my house—I mean, *our* house. I hope you will consent to share it with me."

How strange. I have always thought that house cried out to be filled with children, but I cannot make it that easy for him.

"It is kind of you to offer, but I believe another little matter has slipped your mind."

His brow knitted. "What might that be?"

"Just a trifle. You did not ask me to marry you, so you do

not even know if I will."

"But of course you will. You can do no other—we belong together. I knew that the moment I saw you. I would have married the little governess just as willingly as the difficult countess. Lord knows I haunted that house opposite the pier at every opportunity in the hope that I would see you again. Did you not feel the same way?"

"I took you for a very impudent rascal. No, that is not exactly true. You *were* a rascal. Still are, I am thinking. And yes, I probably do have a soft spot in my heart for such creatures. What I appreciated about you is the fact that you could look beyond the outward trappings to see beauty in someone you took to be a very dowdy little governess. But that does not give you the right to presume I will marry you without being given the chance to decide."

John reached for her and pulled her close. "Darling, admit it. The minute you rushed into my arms, wearing that revealing nightrail and reeking of what I take to be French perfume, you were saying *yes* to something."

Althea grimaced. "I knew it was a mistake to listen to my mother."

"Do not believe that for a moment When it comes to matters of the heart, your mother is the wisest person I know." He tied the ribbons on her cloak more securely. "So?"

"So?"

"Will you marry me?" He nibbled her ear. "I shall do my best to make you very happy." He trailed butterfly kisses across her eyes. "Very, very happy."

She sighed. "Your suit is most persuasive, sir."

"May I presume that is a yes?"

"Oh, yes. A thousand times yes."

"Good."

And he sealed the bargain with the loveliest of kisses.

Educating Emily

He taught her the ways of the world, and she taught him the ways of love.

Fated to be sold into a loveless marriage, Emily Walsingham runs away. But when she is rescued by dashing James Garwood, she fall desperately in love. Recognized by James's mother, Emily is declared the perfect wife for him, despite the fact that he has yet to declare his love for her.

When James Garwood agrees to marry Emily, he never expected to be any more than a tolerable companion. But as she proves to be more caring and intelligent than he imagined, a man thought to be incapable of true devotion will learn more than he bargained for about falling in love.

A Kiss For Lucy

Could the wrong woman be the right love?

Rescued from a life of hardship by her wealthy uncle, Lucy Garwood can't escape the shadow of her elitist relatives. She longs to be loved and respected in her own right, but it seems that as an orphan, her place amongst her blueblood family is unlikely to improve—that is until a case of mistaken identity leads to a kiss from a dashing stranger...

Robert Renquist, Duke of Lindorough, is determined to win the heart of the lovely Maude. But in an attempt to sweep her off of her feet with a daring act of passion, it isn't Maude he kisses, but her half-niece instead. Though conscious of his standing in society, Robert can't deny his unmistakable attraction to Lucy, and he'll soon discover there is only one thing more powerful than his noble lineage—love.

The Love-Shy Lord

Their match was impossible, but their love was inevitable.

Too tall for a society woman, Clarissa has no potential suitors—not that she needs any. She only has eyes for Marcus, viscount of Fairfax. But as a steward's daughter, Clarissa is hardly a suitable match for Marcus.

Marcus Ridley is far too appealing—and eligible—for his own good. Restlessly pursued by desperate maidens, his view of women and marriage is skewed. But then he meets Clarissa, who steals his heart with a single kiss.

Suddenly, Marcus can't get Clarissa off of his mind, and the high-society lord finds himself desperate to make the steward's daughter his wife.